GERONIMO's REVENGE

The third book in the "Geronimo's Revenge" trilogy

by Mike Palecek

For Ruby Montoya and Jessica Reznicek
You did it.

For Lee Harvey Oswald, Osama bin Laden, Timothy McVeigh, Mohammed Atta, Sirhan Sirhan, James Earl Ray, Mark David Chapman, James Holmes, Dzhokhar Tsarnaev, Tamerlan Tsarnaev, Adam Lanza, because you didn't do it.
"They" did.
And we know they did.

For Paul Wellstone.
Murdered.

CWG PRESS

Published by CWG Press, 1517 NE 5th Ter #1, Fort Lauderdale, FL 33304
www.cwgpress.com

Cover art by Audrey McNamara

Printed in the U.S.A.

Also by Mike Palecek

<u>Fiction:</u>

SWEAT: Global Warming in a small town, and other tales from the great
American Westerly Midwest

Joe Coffee's Revolution

The Truth

The American Dream

Johnny Moon

KGB

Terror Nation

Speak English

The Last Liberal Outlaw

The Progrrressive Avenger

Camp America

Twins

Iowa Terror

Guests of the Nation

Looking For Bigfoot

A Perfect Duluth Day

American History 101: Conspiracy Nation

Revolution

One Day In The Life of Herbert Wisniewski

Operation Northwoods: the patsy

Red White & Blue

Welcome to Sugar Creek

CRUSHER vs. The Empire

CRUSHER in Wonderland

<u>Non-fiction:</u>

Cost of Freedom (with Whitney Trettien and Michael Annis)

Prophets Without Honor (with William Strabala)

The Dynamic Duo: White Rose Blooms in Wisconsin, Kevin Barrett, Jim
Fetzer & the American Resistance

Nobody Died At Sandy Hook (with Jim Fetzer)

And I Suppose We Didn't Go To The Moon, Either! (with Jim Fetzer)

Nobody Died At Boston, Either (with Jim Fetzer)

America Nuked on 9/11 (with Jim Fetzer)

Nothing that is worth doing can be achieved in a lifetime; therefore we must be saved by hope.
— Reinhold Niebuhr

I like to get drunk and read Harry Potter, I don't like to wear no shoes … pretend I'm Jerry Jeff Walker … and head to church with the dogs in canoes.
— Ike in HOLLYWOOD

As nightfall does not come at once, neither does oppression. In both instances, there is a twilight when everything remains seemingly unchanged. And it is in such twilight that we all must be most aware of change in the air – however slight – lest we become unwitting victims of the darkness.
— Supreme Court Justice William O. Douglas

Now, the Writers' Union is giving out fur hats to its members, according to their importance — reindeer fawn for a foremost writer, marmot for a leading writer, and so on down the line. Anxious to know where he stands in the literary hierarchy, Yefim rushes to the director's office, where he learns the awful truth: his hat is domestic fluffy tomcat.
— Vladimir Voinovich

He must be in a lot of pain.
He won't be doing that again.
Let not another motherfucker cross my path.
I'm feelin' kind of crazy like a psychopath.
And you don't want to cross me
when I feel this way.
— Folk Uke

ONE

"Make it rain."

The Commander In Chief turned to his sitter standing nearby.

All his little friends from around the world sat together in a tight circle right in the roses.

"The sun is in my eyes," one of his little friends had said.

They had all brought with them their favorite toy.

"I can," said the Most Powerful Man On Earth.

"You can't neither."

"Yes. I can."

The Executive Officer, [who deep-down felt he had literally never had not one moment of comfort or repose thus far in life, I'm just sayin'], sat in the dirt in the roses, his hand up to block the bright sunshine. He rubbed his red knees and his nose, let his tired hand drop and squinted with both eyes and went back to his trucks, still wanting some mud to jump with his big yellow dozer and slosh around in.

The standing man turned and walked briskly inside.

Evey sat with her legs crossed, somehow comfortable, on the back porch with the one iron railing where her mother's blood still stained the cement.

Rachel balanced as she snored on the alien Ojibwe blanket on Roswell, the white dappled mare, as she nibbled grass.

Evey texted Korey.

"We're not gonna kill anybody, anymore.

"That was one of Kaitylyn's ideas. We should have done it in the first place."

"I don't know if we'll be able to do anything, even go outside," said Korey.

"Have you been watching TV?"

"We don't *have* TV."

"You can find it on your phone."

Evey found it, what Korey was talking about.

Prince Hope, the new Master of Ceremonies as he was being called, was on national television, every station, every YouTube channel, every Twitter account, all of Facebook. His face showed on every scoreboard in every baseball stadium in America and every time and temperature electronic marquee in front of every bank in every small town.

His face bulged in super close-up, his straw hat, red bow-tie, one-week gentlemanly funk beard.

That deep delivery so perfect, so nuanced, lyrical, cultured, caring, so perfectly Minnesotan and specifically, Saint Paul. The deep, dark eyebrows marking every comma, semi-colon, dash, and ellipsis.

Hope was talking about fortune cookies. Performing an ad for fortune cookies.

"We are being brought to you today by 'Your Good Fortune Cookies,' helping Americans survive since 1993, and also by 'Hoop Dreams Tri-Focals,' you can still be a millionaire sports figure, at any age, anyone can, just put these on."

A giant, silent grey cloud took captive the bright sun and other big clouds shuffled up until the blue sky was barely visible. Rain sheets fogged the big screens and the camera zoomed out, showing the stage, the little front porch, the American flag, the little wooden homemade sign saying "America."

The band played a jazzy "America The Beautiful" as a local poet clomped in high boots on-stage to her spot at the second microphone.

While in Washington, D.C., He Who Cannot Be Named had come in from playing outside since it had begun to drizzle. He sat at the big desk watching Prince Hope on one of the sets and *Price Is Right* on the other.

The Most Powerful Man On Earth didn't need the pillows from The Daughters Of The Slaughter Of The Philippines to see over the desk anymore.

Those around him remarked to each other with elbows to the side how he appeared larger these days. He had grown bigger in everyone's eyes after what he did in The Rose Garden not that long ago.

Evey walked to Roswell and held out her arms for Rachel to drop when it started to sprinkle. They went inside. Evey curled up on a comfy chair by the window where she could watch the video and also the front lane while Rachel shoved "Nernia" into the DVD player and lost herself in her pillow and blanket on the floor.

(*Where is Blake? He was in the last scene in the last book.*)

(Excellent question. He is around. To be heard from.)

The Chief Diplomat had seven to ten days ago been once again out in the roses playing with his trucks and toy soldiers. A bunny hopped up, sniffed one of the toy soldiers, knocked it over and began nibbling on the feet of the plastic green toy soldier carrying the weapon at his chest, his helmet melded to his eyebrows.

The CEO Of America moved, slowly, keeping his eye on the rabbit, grabbing his favorite soldier with his right hand, the soldier with the bayonet, the giant soldier, solid green, his helmet and face and torso and boots one plastic mold of pure American power and will and purpose.

With a motion more decisive and powerful than you might perhaps expect, the Pres'dent brought that green bayonet down into the neck of the bunny rabbit, squirting blood everywhere around, the roses, himself. He pushed down with both hands while the rabbit squealed and screamed and his sitters watched over him, until the big back feet ceased kicking at the dirt.

He left the bayonet in the neck and sat back, flew his green bombers topped with dirt clods on the wings, dropping their payload on the dead cottontail, and not amused any longer, turned to his knees to plow rocks with his dozer, "*Rrrrr, rrrr, rrrrrmmmm!*"

Evey got a text from Korey that said basically there should be more guys in leadership roles in CRUSHER.

"There have traditionally been more women than men in group home work," said Evey.

"I am the leader now," she said.

"Well, it's been another long week in Moon Rock Lake, my hometown, at the end of the empire."

The camera again zoomed in on Hope center stage, sitting

backwards on his wooden chair, microphone at his mouth, straw hat now pushed back on his head.

"My son was a CRUSHER rebel. He was seduced by a beautiful young rebel woman. And he died. And that's no bullshit."

Hope's eyes searched like he was looking for that one special person in a crowded place. He continued.

"And so now I am the MOC, *your* MOC, Ringmaster, Minister OF Truth. Yes, they paid me a lot of money, and I could use it, after the fire, yes, but we need to stop this, this cancer within us. These theoristas."

He held up a book.

Evey put her hand to her mouth as she clearly saw the handmade book, like a fourth-grade project and the hand-drawn cover on construction paper: *The Pothole Diaries*, by Brooke.

"In this we have a look inside," Hope said.

"Inside the heart and the soul and the mind ... of CRUSHER. We find out how they planned the attacks ... he fired out fingers as he held the book in the same hand ... Mayberry, Mary Tyler Moore, Cicely, Oz."

He began to page through the book as the big and little screens showed the faces of Lara, Brooke, Korey, Jim, Rick, Skylar, Morgan, Pete, Ty, Evey, even Kaitylyn.

"I'm not you," said Hope.

"And you're not me. We think, we do things differently. This is America, a free country.

"But in any case, together we are we, and if we fight, together."

A tear ran down his cheek.

"We can defeat this cancer ... and we will live."

The screen popped to a commercial for BIG VERY RED CHEVY TRUCKS, bouncing over big ruts in a country road. A farmhouse and yard show in the background, and a grain elevator.

The truck bed is filled with Army troops in combat gear. The truck stops and all the troops pile out over the sides, singing, "Good God Y'all. Hoooh! What is it good for?"

The big screens and little screens and screens in fancy New York hotel lounges and tiny neighborhood Chicago bars and every home in Early, Iowa, showed Prince Hope at a microphone.

"It is raining outside. It is raining all over America, in New York City, in Arcata, California; in Scottsbluff, Nebraska; Tecumcari, New Mexico; and Anthony, Texas; Cecil, Georgia; Hammond, Indiana; Winter Harbor, Maine.

"I hear it, see it, feel it. Smell it. Petrichor," he said.

"Is the earthy scent produced when rain falls on dry soil. The word is constructed from Greek meaning stone, and the fluid that flows in the veins of the gods in Greek mythology. Petrichor."

He did a commercial for Petrichor Motor Oil, "in the red can, buy a bunch of 'em at a time, with the pop-top lid, just like Grandpa when he was a kid. You'll be glad you did."

Then the stage went dark behind him. One light shined on Prince Hope, the straw hat now serious.

"Minnesota Ice," he said in that voice.

"It's cold.

"It's a drizzly day, Senator Tommy Carmichael is flying from Minneapolis to Eveleth for a funeral. A black van sits in the woods, front tires in a swamp, waiting.

"A druggist from Virginia driving past the van gets a call on his cellphone and the phone squawks like it has never before or since. John in a little hamlet in the woods just below the plane sees his garage door open and close on its own.

"Lake Black Box shines like a mirror, the slight breeze wiping away the fog.

"Inside the plane the senator turns around, flashing that election-winning smile, joking with his wife and daughter and her husband. The two pilots in the private plane talk about hockey and make landing preparations.

"The senator does some quick work in his lap, answering a question from his office in D.C., about the slaughter of rabbits and how he will stand in the way, right in The Rose Garden, upon his return to work on Monday, if he is the only one.

"The cabin lights blink. A look on the senator's face shows

concern. He puts a hand on the pilot's shoulder just as the plane's nose drops and they begin the short but deadly plummet straight down into the northern Minnesota forest.

"The senator forces himself back to his family. There are only split-seconds. They hit, explode, slam face-first, bleed, burn, die, everything in five seconds that cannot be feared because it is so painful that it cannot really be described, or survived.

"The van pulls away, passing the F.B.I. vehicles already on the scene.

"And for hours, for days, for weeks, for years, the other Minnesota senators and congressmen and governor, old friends of Tommy Carmichael, do not mention Senator Tommy Carmichael, because they can't. They cannot make the words come out of their mouth.

"Because they have their lives, their vacations, pontoons, their work, their bars and their food and their families and a warm, cozy place after a hard day and many days sufficiently difficult and satisfying, and the routine works, for them.

"Rabbits are but rabbits.

"Minnesota Ice.

"It's cold.

"*Hoooh! Just saying.*

"And that's the news from Moon Rock Lake, where all the police and soldiers are thugs, all the Democrats and journalists are cowards, and all the Homeland Security, COINTELPRO lone gunmen, are about average."

Many millions of people hold conspiracy theories; they believe that powerful people have worked together in order to withhold the truth about some important practice or some terrible event. A recent example is the belief, widespread in some parts of the world, that the attacks of 9/11 were carried out not by Al Qaeda, but by Israel or the United States. Those who subscribe to conspiracy theories may create serious risks, including risks of violence, and the existence of such theories raises significant challenges for policy and law. The first challenge is to understand the mechanisms by which conspiracy theories prosper; the second challenge is to understand how such theories might be undermined. Such theories typically spread as a result of identifiable cognitive blunders, operating in conjunction with informational and reputational influences. ... Because those who hold conspiracy theories typically suffer from a crippled epistemology, in accordance with which it is rational to hold such theories, the best response consists in cognitive infiltration of extremist groups. Various policy dilemmas, such as the question whether it is better for government to rebut conspiracy theories or to ignore them, are explored in this light.

— Cass Sunstein

We suggest several policy responses that can dampen the supply of conspiracy theorizing, in part by introducing diverse viewpoints and new factual assumptions into the hard-core groups that produce such theories. Our principal claim here involves the potential value of cognitive infiltration of extremist groups, designed to introduce informational diversity into such groups and to expose indefensible conspiracy theories as such.

— Cass Sunstein

TWO

I was returning from a family wedding and thinking how things had changed and it was very possible that I would not die a hero, known to all. I know what I'd really like though even more than that, and that would be to always be with friends and family, loved, comfortable. But the wars will not allow that. You have to fight them or what are you? You are one of them and you just said you want nothing but to be like them, liked by them, but yeah, you know what I mean. And the wars make it impossible to be there, where you want to be. You have to be different and both will not be allowed. You have to be resigned to this version of life. The kind Jesus had, split from childhood friends, family, no real fucking job, his own little family, house. I mean not that any of us is fucking Jesus, it's just that it seems like it works out that way, right? So, you come a long way to Cana for a wedding, and you go back a long ways as well.

I grow up thinking I am special, all those thoughts and observations that go along with that and I go to a staff work day and there is a special day on "types" and find there is already a clinical term for me. I am not a hero. I am a personality disorder. It has been there all along. And I think, of course I am.

Sometimes you have to throw up before you can feel better.

I'm thinking of stopping talking.

There is nobody for me to talk to, nothing for me to say. If you know what I mean I feel sorry for you. You go to the workout place, into the gas station, to church, to bowl. You try at first, of course, you always try, but then you see a chair by the wall and you sit in it. You know it was put there for you.

You rest your elbows on your knees like the young girl at the dance who was perfectly happy at home reading, and you realize, not out of despair or panic, but calmly, there is nothing you know how to say that will enter you into these scenes. In this play you have no lines and you wonder maybe I don't even care anymore.

Well, The BIM (h), Josie Marsha Marsha Marsha Custer is

still in court. She already had the lawyer paid for with something called pre-paid legal insurance? She had another day coming, even after Kaitylyn, and she wanted to get the use of it.

She kept thinking about "the ticket," that thing Geronimo found in the shred room and he kept, the ticket to one of the planes on 9/11. And, she knew it had to have fingerprints. There would have been Geronimo, Korey, Jim, Kaitylyn and one more. The thing was to find out who that other one was, and that could be the thing to find out who really murdered Gerry, Geronimo, Napoleon Ulysses Custer. She never actually saw the ticket, but she knew. She knew whose fingerprints were all over this.

So, that's happening.

Did you know that Omah is a word for Bigfoot and so one might assume that Omaha is named after Bigfoot. And do you know how many places, sites, just in the United States, are named "Devil." Devil something. A lot. And one might guess that is also because of Bigfoot. You could.

Did you know that it is assumed or guessed by some that one of our Presidents robbed the actual Geronimo's grave so that his club could have the bones in their dark little meeting room, for fun?

Do you know what a spirit quest is? I'm not sure, but I think it's something to do with a sweat lodge. You do a bunch of shit and some spirit in the form of an animal comes to you in your fucking hallucination and then that is your spirit animal for the rest of your life. Not sure what fucking good that does, but anyway.

Okay, well, here we go. It's time for court now.

We are gathered again in the local federal court.

Josie is there, and her lawyer, and the judge and her goons.

The lawyer has asked the court to obtain the fingerprints of any agents of the federal government who have been stationed in the Twin Cities over the past five to ten years.

The government has fought that and today we find out if the judge will make them do it or whether she will just drop the whole fucking thing.

I work with a group of researchers who have been working this case from the day it happened. The official story states only two [2] bombs going off, and both of these can be seen and determined to be smoke bombs. The first one even pre-announced in a tweet by the Boston Globe as a "drill" – so I have to come to the conclusion that as there are only two bombs reported that there cannot have been any real victims – that is, aside from the two patsies that were framed and convicted by MSM.

"cui prodest scelus, is fecit":

I see this as a beta-test for the Martial Law Template. The whole reason for this act was the establishment of the Gestapo crackdown, to take the temperature of the public
as far as going along with the police state tactics that ensued in the aftermath.

— James Petras

I will stand with my brothers and sisters. I will tell the truth about them and about why we went to Wounded Knee. I will fight for my people. I will live for them, and if it is necessary to stop the terrible things that happen to Indians on the Pine Ridge Reservation, I am ready to die for them.

But the judge and his lawyers must know by now I will never lie against my people, crawl for a better deal for myself.

I stand with Russell Means, Gladys Bissonette, Carter Camp, Ellen Moves Camp, Clyde Bellecourt...

— an affidavit presented to the court on June 27, 1973 by Pedro Bissonette

THREE

$B_{ill,}$

I am a painter, have been and will be. I agree the information we get is a thin tissue of lies. My painting, like T.G., has a rabid following in the high single digits. The rest are indifferent. Fuck'em.

Maybe time will redeem us.

ALL REALITY IS A THIN TISSUE OF LIES.

Steve,

Perhaps you read yesterday's note to Bix. For you or Bix or whoever may have, I should report that I did better against the lines of tiniest ant I have seen, than thought yesterday. I was in bed trying to read, and they bite, and I killed them between thumb and forefinger and with plenty insect repellant.

Last night I slept better than I had past couple or three nights, and today they are not on my bed.

A species of ant will telegraph its own kind someway. Fireants - several or more sizes larger than this species - attacked me in grand waves, maybe 2 years, but seem gone from inside the trailer this past year. The other problem this year thus far is asthma has not given enough rest for me to not take Aprodine decongestants day/night with drink.

Certain decongestants became a controlled substance, Actifed, Aprodine. One has to present driver's license and sign and is allowed not enough. Am not sure where this is going, plus I am fat. Either event, now even I with laptop can get "Alternate News" and study direction of puny man. Talking about lies, yall. I wade slowly. Then drain the swamp, yall. Shoot Boy Trump for being incoherent. How can he escape like Obama. Shoot him for an unpredictable and dangerous fat child age 70. Too late for him. Steve, when somebody becomes a USA president, he quickly is told something. From the "Deep State," lately called this. Next, the new president is disturbed. He falls in line. Obama bombed the most innocents, imprisoned the most Whistle Blowers. JFK had independence and guts and was taken out for this. Last president with any humanitarian values was Carter and his administration committed horrors in Latin America and he escaped still alive after a single term. Solace is the Net pulls in enough talk for anyone bored with an infantile circus. A thinker can get enough of it. Looks to me like suddenly there are too many thinkers to kill or imprison. I need to go get some protein. I have this regular pot of beans and salt pork where I tossed later on in a couple pounds of beef heart. I have to stay dangerous.

Good to hear from you. Either event, Bill

Bill was not in the state mental hospital in the country outside of so-called Bumfuck, Iowa when Korey went there last.

I'm wondering if the aliens took him up in their spacecraft or if he just dreamed up the aliens. But then who gave that Ojibwe Dancing Alien blanket to Roswell, is what I'm wondering, if not the aliens. We're talking about "The Callwell Boys," with the giant feet they seem self-conscious about and the potty-mouth names.

But he is back communicating with his friends and his family, by his blog, by email, hand-written letter, something.

So, your guess is as good as mine at this point.

Maybe Korey didn't go to the right mental hospital?

I just dunno.

QUOTE REMOVED BY ORDER OF DHS, UNITED STATES
DEPARTMENT OF HOMELAND SECURITY. [DHS US2FA]

I'm afraid, based on my own experience, that fascism will come to America in the name of national security.

— Jim Garrison

FOUR

The judge, Marlene Baurmeister, was already waiting when everyone else started to wander in. So we all hurried to get situated and there was no chit-chat. The lawyers left their briefcases and folders unopened on the tables.

Judge Baurmeister: We are here today to talk about the ticket.

Josie's lawyer: Yes, your honor. We ask that the prints on the ticket be matched against certain federal employees of that time.

Government lawyer (Ms. Coffman): We object. There's too many. How do we do that?

Judge Baurmeister: Fingerprints? You do that all the time.

Government lawyer: I don't.

Judge Bauermeister: Somebody does.

Government lawyer: Yes, but. That's a lot of time and expense, not to mention taking these people away from their work. And, we are not going to gather the other side's evidence for them.

Judge Baurmeister: You will obtain them, both of you.

Josie's lawyer: That will take a lot of work.

Judge: And whose side are you on? Are you withdrawing your request?

Josie's lawyer: No, just sayin'.

One month later Judge Bauermeister's court gathered again.

Josie's attorney said there had been a match.

"Carroll," she said. "Just Carroll."

The government attorney, Ms. Coffman then objected that how can there be a match when we do not have the actual ticket.

Judge Bauermeister shot daggers at Josie's attorney to say WTF!

"Yes, your honor," said Josie's attorney what's-her-name, "we don't have the actual ticket."

"Then how can there ever be a match, might I ask?" said the judge.

"What we have," said Josie's lawyer, is something in the law called suspension of disbelief and we believe we have prints that might have been involved, in fact one set of prints."

"That is not a legal term," said the judge, "it is a theatrical term and you are out of your element."

Josie's lawyer quickly explained while the government lawyer smirked and started to gather her papers that while they did not yet have the actual ticket they did have a manifesto which was found in Geronimo's room and it had many fingerprints on it, including those of Carroll.

"But we cannot find him. He's in the C.I.A.," said Josie's lawyer, pushing on.

"I know right where he is," said the judge.

She pointed.

"Right there. I know him."

She commanded Carroll to get on the stand.

Josie's attorney asked him how his fingerprints came to be on the American Airlines ticket for that flight (175 ?) for Sept. 11, 2001.

The courtroom went silent as Josie's lawyer recognized her error and backtracked to say manifesto rather than ticket.

Carroll smiled, remaining silent. He motioned for the government attorney to approach him.

"It's a matter of national security," the attorney said upon returning to her position.

"The hell it is," said the judge.

"Take him into custody for contempt of court," she commanded the two large men standing near her.

They continued to stand, hands at their waist, staring silently into the crowd.

"Oh, for Christ's sake," said the judge.

"Recess, until one p.m. I'll get to the bottom of this."

Most everyone left the courtroom at that time.

Some few stayed. I watched the judge working with papers then turning to go into the door behind her. I watched the government lawyers gather their shit and click out on the hard floor, then Josie's lawyer, then Josie. She waved to me and left, all dressed in Indian lore and jewelry to the nine, with that tomahawk on her side, surprised they let her have it, probably didn't notice it with all the other jingle dress, braids, ear rings, high boots bead shawl goin' on.

They went, I followed, noticed how the big goons waited with hands folded until I finally left, out into the big, airy marble floor dome area, with all the other light and plants and doors running off this big circle, the kind of government building architecture that makes you think somebody really thought about this whole government thing, it means something.

Carroll was out there, in the middle, waiting, standing on some image inlayed into the floor and he must have been waiting for Josie because as soon as she came out he walked toward her, large confident clicks of those shiny shoes, the big smile already all over his face, grey hair shining in the sun coming through a million windows.

It was all so nice, so symmetrical, acoustic, where a footstep from over there sounded like it was right here, even in tennis shoes or moccasins.

She kept going, her bells jingling, and they were bound to meet like a submarine intersecting with a destroyer.

They closed on each other, each still striding not slowing. He began to reach out his shaking hand.

She placed the tomahawk in the middle of his forehead like a hatchet into a melon, so quickly, smoothly.

It didn't bleed, not yet.

Geezuz god his head thumped on that hard, shined fancy floor.

His lips turned blue and his pink face faded to grey. His blue eyes froze in that moment he saw the tomahawk.

Now the blood spilled out — geezuz fuck — puddling around his head, mixing with the grey hair that had remained neat and perfect with the hairspray from the tiny expensive canister, the good stuff.

I recalled how she had told me once something of the history of that tomahawk.

How it had been her father's, grandfather's and passed on to him from his father, going back to the wars against the Dakota at The Battle of the Brule, The U.S Cavalry, even taken into The Battle of the Bulge, Little Bighorn.

QUOTE REMOVED BY ORDER OF DHS, UNITED STATES
DEPARTMENT OF HOMELAND SECURITY. [DHS US2FA]

Richard Dolan:

"The moment of disclosure [UFOs] is not the end
of anything, it's the beginning of the
real fight for truth.

We saw demonstrations of a million people in
Tahrir Square ... don't you think there might be a
march of a million people on Area 51, Wright Patter-
son Air Force Base, Los Alamos ... maybe ... I'll bet
you Wackenhut Security can stop a march of a hundred people, but not a million, not a million.

And don't you think that just might happen.

And what about opening up a
new truth movement?

Because ... after UFOs, then 9/11, JFK, underground bases, you name it, chemtrails, it's all going
to be on the table.

By God, what an exciting, challenging, mess
it's going to be.

And so in other words, the moment of disclosure
is not going to be the end of anything ...
it's the beginning for the real fight for truth.

Not the end.

FIVE

 By now the fancy red Suburbans were beat to shit.

Alice, Charlie, Frida, and Ike sat on the highway below the HOLLYWOOD sign on a steep hill with bumps and rocks and cactus and burrs.

(We do all recall? That they left the Twin Cities after the Wonderland debacle? To attack Hollywood, as it were, for its maleficence in polluting the public mind, as someone put it, not me.)

"Woah," said Alice.

"Yahoo!" shouted Actually, who had come along as a special advisor, but he needed to get back ASAP. He was getting daytime hours at White Castle and was not going to screw up his promotion.

"Woah," said Ike, seeing all the details of the terrain not visible from the road.

Charlie was driving.

"Oh, well," he said, cranking the steering wheel.

They went down first into a little gully, then up the other side and right onto the steep hill.

Charlie gunned it. The tires spun like a dune buggy. He dropped into second and then low and all sorts of things ground and whined and hissed. The others rolled their windows down and stuck their arms and heads out the windows.

"Yahoo!"

Over bumps they flew, throwing up rocks and film canisters, old L.A. Times movie reviews, memorandums on C.I.A. letterhead, F.B.I. rubber stamps, cast photos, marching orders for Charlie Manson, a Folger's can from RALPH's (marked "Donnie"), Eddie Haskell's white tennis shoes, wine bottles, black and white photos of Ben Affleck, cigar boxes, Mark Wahlberg, Johnny Carson, Jimmy Stewart, in manila envelopes stamped "Classified."

The HOLLYWOOD sign grew bigger and bigger above them, a giant gorilla, a lizard.

They made it just as something clunked, something banged and the engine stopped.

They worked to encircle the sign with a sandbag bunker and dig down, encamp. They looked out over their hill and the highway and the traffic with their AR-15s and their binoculars, searching for the assault and the helicopters and the fighter jets.

"I'm not sure anyone can see us," said Alice, "we're pretty small, actually."

She smiled and pointed at Actually.

"I'll go look," said Ike and Frida went with him.

They crawled down the hill and stood by the highway, looking up at the HOLLYWOOD sign and the CRUSHER occupying force.

"Can kinda see ya," Ike said as he talked to Charlie by phone.

"Wave your arms."

Those on the hill waved their hands over their heads and shouted.

"Nope, nothing," said Ike.

"Well, shit," he said, looking at Frida.

Frida shrugged her shoulders.

They climbed back up the hill, really a mountain, and everyone helped them to crawl over and into the bunker, got them water as they lay sweating and puffing.

"Really?" said Charlie. "Nothing? A little?"

Ike nodded his head, held up his fingers close together, closed his eyes and rested back against one of the legs of the "H."

This was just what Actually had expected. He jumped the barricade and dashed for the red Suburban. He took a few trips to haul all the crap he had brought with him.

"Was ist das alles gut fur?" said Frida, who was trying to learn German for whatever reason.

"Huh?" said Actually.

"What's all this?"

"Oh, well, let me show you," said Actually.

And he demonstrated how with this equipment they would be able to broadcast their own radio station and be picked up in parts of Hollywood and some of the cars going past.

"Couldn't we just do a YouTube channel?" said Ike.

"Yeaaah, you *couuuld*," said Actually, "but this is way cooler, actual radio, they won't expect it. It's bad-ass."

"Yeah, it actually is," said Alice, and she high-fived with Actually.

"CRUSHER 2.0," said Charlie.

So, that night they sat at a card table that had fit in quite nicely, actually, in the Suburban, made level by digging and by sandbags and by plywood found on the hill, they broadcast their first show.

They took turns reading from the script Actually has provided from Max.

"I think Max wrote this a while ago," he said.

(Actually)

… And now … we join … in progress … another episode of "The Americans."

"The Americans" is brought to us each week by "Adventures in Mein Homeland," publishers of vetted newspapers, novels and magazines since 1948.

(Ike)

Also sponsored by "MK-Ultra Torture Depends." "When you're getting your ass beat and your balls stomped, we're there for you. Let it fly. We'll catch it." … MK-Ultra Torture Depends.

(Frida)

Also by "Left Behind Depends," for the conservative Christian who does not get raptured up and just doesn't know why, we're there for you.

(Alice)

Also by "Black Site Depends," for the American international traveler.

(Charlie)

Also by Crisis Actors Of The Homeland, Operation Mockingbird, Operation Northwoods, COINTELPRO, and by Craft and Blackwater, bringing you the Boston bombing, Sandy Hook, San Bernardino and so much more.

(Actually)

And now, "The Americans," …

It's true that the newcomers to Washington, D.C. are different than ever before … but after all is said and done … they are Americans.

We return to our story.

(Frida)

The construction is underway for the wall around the Washington, D.C. Beltway … to separate The White House, the FBI, the CIA, the Pentagon, the Congress and the Washington Press Corps from normal human beings.

Scattered around the job site are the wooden boards to be tacked up all around the new wall with the message, "Let me put it this way: while 9/11 was a US "deep state" operation (probably subcontracted for execution to the Israelis), the entire Washington 'swamp' has been, since 9/11, accomplice after the fact, by helping to maintain the cover-up. If this is brought into light, then thousands of political careers are going to crash and burn into the scandal." [Saker]

(Ike)

And we find newly elected Pres'dent Cosmo Nutt dressed in business camo, seated behind his big desk in The Parallelogram Office at his Big Desk doodling on his big yellow legal pad … with not much to do, one finger on the red nuclear button and, with his right hand, drawing some last-minute dollar signs, boobs and tanks before he has to go down to greet the something-something of some little pygmy country.

(Frida)

There is a child hiding behind the curtains, looking out, wondering – a child left behind by the previous people, perhaps the previous people to that.

(Actually)

Slappy The House Alien is just now going outside to feed the Secretary of Defense in the kennel.

(Alice)

Juice The Limo Driver adjusts his yarmulke, waiting to

take the president to Camp Verl in the woods for a weekend meeting with Toad, the new Vice-President, and his wife, Toaddette.

(Charlie)
Meanwhile ...
Tom, The All-American Sniper, sits on his bench on the Chesapeake & Ohio Canal towpath.

He's wearing his brown Boy Scout sash with badges he has earned.

He's got his gun right there with him on the bench on this glorious bright morning.

(Ike)
Every once in a while he will pop a bird on the water or a walker on the sidewalk across the water. People come up to him and point and say he did it.

He says, no I didn't, and is always left alone, to continue shooting and killing.

(Charlie)
Buzz the space dog is wearing casual camo and is showing Ricardo the space cat the moon set ... and showing how it will all work for Ricardo to be the quote first cat on the moon in This New Exciting Era.

(Frida)
Ricardo is so freaking stupid, unconcerned with nuance, just wanting to look good.

Buzz is from the old school when fake really meant something.

(Alice)
Outside the fence The Protester sits as he has for decades. He uses the same signs, just crosses out names and puts in the new names.

He has his signs spread out across the sidewalk and sometimes a tourist will look or take a picture.

(Actually)

Join us next week for another episode of "The Americans" when we will look in on The Big Formal Camo Ball.

"That should do it," said Actually.

[– Richard Dolan - Talking about seeing kids at a playground.]

Would these children know they live in a fascist society? Would their parents know they live in a fascist society? Is it possible to live in a fascist society without realizing it? Of course it's possible.

When you talk about facism people instinctively talk about Hitler and Mussolini and brown shirts and walking goose-step down the streets. That's fascism that's in your face. Of course, it doesn't have to be like that. That's not the defining feature. Fascism can be sexy. Fascism can look like American Idol or Monday Night Football, Internet video games, or whatever, it can be the things that distract you the citizen from what's actually going on. Fascism, in other words, can be a lot more attractive, than they realize, to people.

… What we have is invisible fascism. It's fascism that people can't really see, frankly because most people don't have the conceptual tools to understand what's happened.

Most people have to work, they've got families, they've got things to do, they're not out there to fight the machine, they're not out there to be heroes, they're just out there to live their lives. They don't want to have trouble. They haven't really studied this matter. They may feel in their bones that there's something wrong. Sure they do.

But it's one thing to feel there's something wrong and it's another to be able to put it all together and to conceptualize it and to see how it's wrong.

So, I see what has happened is that it's a fascism
that you can feel, but you can't see it, because you
don't know how to see it, that's why
I call it invisible.

That's what we have. In other words, for us to assume that today fascism is going to look like Hitler's
fascism, well that's kind of stupid. We're living in a
completely different century, a completely different
era. Of course it's not going to look like Hitler's fascism. It's going to look very different. …

9/11 plays a crucial part in allowing that …

… because what was necessary was to have a
legal revolution within the United States.

And that of course, is what has 9/11 has allowed.
… It has also allowed a fascist revolution. What else
do we call it? It has gone under the radar as such.

— Richard Dolan

SIX

Actually and the others had no idea.

Their broadcast had not only gone out to the cars passing below them on the highway, but to practically every computer and radio in America. Their vantage on the high steep hill at the foot of the HOLLYWOOD sign was the perfect place because of the many antennas shoved in the tops of the letters in the giant sign, as well as the breeze blowing in off the ocean, the perfect serendipitous positioning of the red Suburban where it sat on the hill in relation to the sign and the wires and the antennas... Maybe also due to sun spots, moon shadows, crop squares, and a sudden unreported increase in Bigfoot sightings, and because Actually was the kind of genius he was, guessing the diode he had invented might allow their signal to bounce everywhere on the thousands of cell phone towers everywhere.

If he did not have to work at White Castle he probably would have invented something. That's what he told himself, but he just didn't have the time these days, not with that manager position within reach.

While in fact, he just had.

He had invented the first nationwide underground clandestine radio show underneath the "H" in HOLLYWOOD. He just didn't know it.

Prince Hope heard the show, mysteriously coming from the speakers in the theater as he stood alone at the podium, writing, thinking, and he was not happy because he thought some of the bits sounded familiar. The Pres'dent listened on the toy radio still stuck in the mud in the rose garden, and it still worked, as he played with his new toy with the yellow plastic nametag on his yellow plastic shirt: BOB.

The following morning it rained.

Prince Hope's giant face showed behind the rain on every screen, every cellphone, everything.

He talked about the man, Bob, who robbed the gun store

and taped to the window of the gun store a manifesto, a letter in which he called for revolution and called himself a revolutionary. He wandered through the gun store looking plainly like, according to the commentators regarding the CCTV that we never saw, a white man radicalized on the internet.

"He then roared off in his vehicle into the night, changing forever the landscape of America," said the TV newswoman. "Because, frankly, we will never know quite where he is at any particular moment. He could be anywhere, anyone."

"Anyone who uses those antiquated terms today is an enemy of freedom," said Hope, meaning revolution and revolutionary, rain dripping off his stylish straw cap and his beard, making him look to some like a Venezuelan game show host during the rainy season.

"Are you kidding me? Revolution? Revolutionary? In these days? When we have to do all we can just to maintain freedom? Anyone who calls himself a revolutionary is a selfish fool concerned only with himself.

"We wonder if he is one of the CRUSHER group."

Thus began the nationwide search, door to door, for Bob, labeled immediately that afternoon in the junior high history books and Trivial Pursuit as The Great Exploration.

City police, state troopers, F.B.I. agents, National Guard troops went door to door all over the country. It was advertised as more like selling Girl Scout Cookies, but many were roughed up in the massive project, taking people out of their homes, farm houses and apartments, into the front yard while they searched the home.

Evey, Blake and Rachel waited nervously by the mailbox, in the steady drizzle, holding every belonging they could carry, waiting for Korey and Washington to get there after hitchhiking from The Cities.

"How much longer, mommy?" says Rachel.

"Not that much," says Evey, hugging her close to her side and softly singing, *"des colores, des colores ... es el arco ... iris que vemos lucir ..."*

"Here we go," said Blake.

The smoke showed someone coming. And then more smoke the other way.

They waited anxiously and smiled when the first smoke cloud to arrive carried within it, like the good witch in the soap bubble, Korey and Washington.

They scampered into the woods across the road and watched as three National Guard trucks stormed the drive, clattering, one right on the tail of the other, barely fitting on the little path.

They watched from the woods as the troops rushed the front door and encircled the building, stomped around the yard as if trying to kill all the nightcrawlers and a little way into the shelter belt. Evey spied Roswell's face among the branches. A soldier peed in the yard and Evey quick put her hand over Rachel's eyes.

The soldiers, in desert camo, stood around in the yard for a while. An eagle flew over, swooping. One soldier aimed his weapon at the bird, then put the gun down.

At an unseen order the troops walked back to the vehicles and climbed aboard. The trucks backed out, the transmissions whining, then roared away on the dirt road.

So, do we go back to the house or head on?

That was the unsaid question that hung in the air in the hiding place in the woods.

"They won't probably come back, now," said Blake.

"I don't know how that works," said Korey.

"They might think we're gone now and will come back later," said Evey.

"I doubt they have time to come back," said Washington.

Then another truck came racing in. Rumbling, loud, throwing up dust and rocks, making a sharp turn into the lane. These soldiers jumped down, shooting, hooting and hollering.

"Hoooh!"

Some sprinted into the woods shooting. Some ran into the house. Shots popped and glass broke.

"Oh my God," said Evey.

"This is crazy," said Blake.

"This way," said Korey, turning away into the woods.

They walked, tromped and stumbled, through the trees, for what seemed like miles. They came to a dirt road, crossed it, kept going. Blake carried Rachel on his shoulders and she had to duck branches. Evey held Rachel for a ways, then Washington, then Korey, then Rachel walked herself .

The little group, burrs in their hair, so alone in the big world, hungry, thirsty, shoved through thick bushes and found themselves in the back alley of a small town.

Someone came out a back door, tossing a bag into the garbage, a whistling space alien wearing jeans, tennis shoes, t-shirt.

The person stared at the group as if not believing what he was seeing.

The big alien head person cautiously walked across the alley.

"Who are you?" he said.

"Who are we?" said Evey.

She could see over the alien head person other people walking on main street, also with alien heads.

"Why aren't you wearing your heads?" said the person.

"Heads?" said Blake as Rachel put both hands on her head.

"For Paranormal-Not Normal Days. Of course."

"Is that what this is?" said Evey. "Where have we landed?"

"The Twilight Zone," mumbled Korey.

"Lake Wobegon," said the voice inside the alien mask with no lips moving.

"Wawakane," it added.

"Oh my God," Evey put both hands to her face.

They walked the little path between two buildings to main street.

Everywhere were banners and flags and ribbons, moon flags, Mars flags, Jupiter, and across the street a giant banner with space ship images said PARANORMAL-NOT NORMAL DAYS.

All around them people ambled past and stared at the little group. The others wore alien heads, Bigfoot heads and children shot little ghost whisps out of spray cans that could be purchased today only with the money going to the local Historical Society.

They walked, slowly, Evey, Rachel, Blake, Korey, Washington, trying to take it all in. Over there was the carnival, there was the park, the ball field, and there, right in front of the city offices, a bronze statue. Evey headed right for it.

"Ohmygod."

It was a smiling Rachel, holding out a pie to passersby, whom she had killed. She touched it with one fingertip. It was hard, solid, substantial, not going anywhere.

"Let's keep moving," said Blake.

They sat to rest on a bench in front of the newspaper building and listened to music coming from somewhere, the do-do, do-do, do-do intro music to *The Twilight Zone*.

"I know you," said an inquisitive Wookie with a notepad and camera. "Don't I know you?"

"No, you don't," said Blake, putting his arm around Evey and trying to bounce a skeptical Rachel on his knee.

"I know you," insisted the Wookie, now on one knee, taking off its head, and shaking off long hair, wiping a sweaty face with a hair arm.

"Your tattoos," said Abby Inquvist.

"I thought I recognized you."

"Listen," said Blake, "we really don't want any …"

"Can we do an interview?" said Abby.

"No," said Evey at the same time that Korey said, "sure."

"This is new," said Abby. "My idea actually. It's a time when we can be free, all these police around lately, everywhere. And, it's a way to say these are not normal days we are having in the country. So far the police don't get the connection."

"I know, right?" said Rachel with a pirate smile.

"You are so cute, dear," said Abby.

"What's your name?"

"Rachel," said Evey.

"Oh, yeah, I see," said Abby.

"Yeah," whispered Evey.

Abby sat and visited for a while. They didn't talk about the attack on the July 4th parade or the first Rachel, though she did mention the graveyard in passing when talking about her own grandmother who had died not that long ago.

"Listen," she said.

Korey showed Washington how he could spit cool out of his missing tooth.

"Obviously, you're not a golfer," whispered Washington.

"We need to fight this," said Abby.

They understood.

"Okay," said Evey, deciding to be one of the brave, at the same time that Blake sucked his lips and took a deep breath.

They got up, turned around and followed Abby into the newspaper office.

Abby nodded to a man in a black suit and Darth Vader head sitting on an uncomfortable wooden chair by the door, reading the latest issue.

They headed straight for the way back by the web press and developing room.

The story ran on the front page the next week, showing Evey, Blake, Rachel, Korey, Washington, all in alien heads and wearing CRUSHER t-shirts that Abby had found out in the park and around town the day of the July 4th attack.

Prince Hope's face showed on every screen everywhere.

He wore a Saint Paul Saints blue and white ball cap turned around backward and the towel around his neck and the sweat intimated he might have just come back from jogging or playing tennis.

He was clean shaven and had taken to whitening his teeth, very, scary white.

"It is amazing watching the American people come together and being so welcoming in allowing law enforcement to do their jobs and for those officers of the law who put in long hours away from their families to make sure America is made safe again.

"Thanks go out to citizens for putting out their guns on the lawn where the people have put them and law enforcement takes them away for safe keeping so that they do not come into "the wrong hands at the wrong time."

He reminded everyone that the Boy Scouts and Girl Scouts would continue their Saturday morning free gun pickup for the next three weeks and that after that it will be on an on-call basis and there will be a small fee attached to gun pickup.

"But then we have this."

He held up the front page of *The Lake Wobegon/Wawakane Weekly Reminder* with the four-column photo of the CRUSH-ERs in alien head repose on the bench on main street.

"They are still out there," said Hope so seriously, sadly.

"Enemy of the people," he said, putting on thick black glasses, the tip of his nose and reading something.

"That is what CRUSHER means in Ojibwe."

"No it doesn't," said Abby out loud, watching the TV on her exercise bike in the Lake Wobegon/Wawakane Anytime Fitness.

"And we in Minnesota trust our ancestors. They understood what truth really means.

"CRUSHER. Enemy of the people."

"Well, it does now," said Abby, pushing down and grunting, at the same time trying to switch the channel with the remote, getting only Prince Hope everywhere.

And then he held up a Coke can, said "drink Coca-Cola," and then every screen everywhere switched to a commercial for "Big Red Chevy Pickups, Really Really Red."

One of the great mysteries of the Vietnam War era has been solved. On March 8, 1971, a group of activists — including a cab driver, a day care director and two professors — broke into an FBI office in Media, Pennsylvania. They stole every document they found and then leaked many to the press, including details about FBI abuses and the then-secret counter-intelligence program to infiltrate, monitor and disrupt social and political movements, nicknamed COINTELPRO. They called themselves the Citizens' Commission to Investigate the FBI. No one was ever caught for the break-in. The burglars' identities remained a secret until this week when they finally came forward to take credit for the caper that changed history. Today we are joined by three of them — John Raines, Bonnie Raines and Keith Forsyth; their attorney, David Kairys; and Betty Medsger, the former Washington Post reporter who first broke the story of the stolen FBI documents in 1971 and has now revealed the burglars' identities in her new book, "The Burglary: The Discovery of J. Edgar Hoover's Secret FBI."

In the first part of our discussion, we talked about how March 8th, 1971, went down, the night of the Joe Frazier-Muhammad Ali fight, using that as a cover because it would be a lot of noise and the belief that the guards would be watching this in the Media offices. But there was criticism leveled—or you feared there would be, John and Bonnie Raines—of why you did this, because you could have gone to jail for many, many years. You had three kids under 10. Professor John Raines, what was your thinking process leading up to this?

JOHN RAINES:

Sure, that's a great question. We were the only ones, out of the eight, who were not only husband and wife, but father and mother of three children under 10. And we were not into the being a martyr. We were not into jeopardizing the future of our children. We were pretty sure—if we weren't pretty sure, we wouldn't have, in fact, gone into that office and taken out those files. So we were pretty sure we could get away with it.

But the second thing that's important to know is that we routinely ask, as a society, mothers and fathers to take on as part of their work highly dangerous kinds of activities. We ask that of all policemen. We ask that of everybody that works for the fire department. We ask that of mothers and fathers who are stationed overseas, sent overseas to defend our freedoms in the Army and Navy. We routinely ask of people to take on jobs that risk their families. Now, we were faced back in 1971 with nobody in Washington was going to do what had to be done if we were going to reveal what J. Edgar Hoover was doing with his FBI. We were the last line of defense. So, as citizens, we stepped forward and did what we had to do because nobody in Washington would do what they should have done. Then, after we did what we did, people in Washington, with the help of Betty's revealing stories in the Post, then they began, finally, to oversee J. Edgar Hoover's FBI, and things changed.

— *Democracy Now*

SEVEN

At the HOLLYWOOD sign, in California, Actually feverishly, intuitively, sincerely worked his ipad Notebook to Google "how to use radio for revolution."

"I'm getting nothing," he said to Charlie.

"It should work. Everything is in there. Try adding something," said Charlie, "maybe you're being too general, be more specific, yeah, actually try that."

So, yeah, Actually then searched for "how to use radio for revolution, up the hill off the highway, right under the HOLLYWOOD sign."

"Nothin'," he said.

"Wait," Actually said.

"And he added, "with sandbags for bunkers."

"Bingo," he said, smiling, looking over at Charlie who was watching traffic with the binoculars trying to spot anyone with a really surprised look on their face from getting the rebel broadcast right on their car radio.

After the interview in the newspaper office they walked out of town, the back way.

"This way," said Evey as she headed off the little road into the woods.

For hours they tromped, through swamp, over giant downed trees with big root balls and root ball caves perfect for hiding, or living, into and out of thick brush, branches in their eyes and in their gut.

"This way," said Evey as she headed up a little hill.

"Finally," said Washington.

"What?" he said as Evey crossed a paved highway and disappeared into the woods on the other side.

They followed her, Rachel on Blake's shoulders, Korey, Washington, keeping her orange T-shirt in sight and sometimes not in the thick northern Minnesota underbrush.

"Are there bears here?" said Washington.

"Yes," said Blake.

"Oh, good. Wolves?"

"Yep," said Korey.

"Perfect," said Washington.

"Bigfoot," mumbled Korey and he was pretty sure nobody heard, which was fine.

They found Evey stopped at a rock wall.

"Here we go," she said, parting the branches and stepping in, then pausing and looking back over her shoulder with a smile, "You are now leaving America, no passports required … Narnia, Oz, Wonderland … the Iron Range," and then she walked straight into the rock and was gone.

"What'd she say?" Washington asked Korey. Korey shrugged and gave Washington a little shove.

"I don't know, go on, go," said Korey.

They followed, pushing aside the hanging green tarp with " Beware Of Dragon" in white paint.

It was dark, right away. Think of really dark and that's it.

So they stopped, hearing Evey scratching around, searching.

"It's here," she said, still looking, "somewhere."

Then the lights came on, not bright, but they could see.

"I couldn't find the switch," she said.

The underground had been wired, they marveled, thankful, still needing to watch their step, it was not great fucking light, but they could fucking see.

They walked down and around and sideways, slowly, pausing at a kitchen area, a sleeping quarters, a rec room with radio and bean bag.

"Viet Cong," said Evey, lovingly touching a wall.

"What's?" Washington looked back at Korey.

"Just keep it moving," Korey gave Washington just a little shove.

"Look at this," said Blake.

They gathered around markings on the wall. One drawing a fist with the middle finger sticking up.

"Reuben," said Evey, putting a hand over Rachel's eyes.

"Hey," said Washington, pointing at what looked like a

spaceship, round and below it little things with big heads and big feet.

"They look like they lost something on the ground. They're looking down," said Korey.

"It looks like main street on …," said Washington.

"Wawakane-Wobegon," said Evey.

"Yeah," said Washington.

"There's a reporter."

Washington pointed at a Bigfoot-looking figure.

"Bigfoot," said Blake, "Sa'be to the Ojibwe."

"They must have …" said Korey.

"Had 'em up here way back then," said Washington.

"Wonder where they went to."

"Up in the spaceship," said Blake.

"Still here," whispered Evey.

"Still here," said Rachel.

They found another kitchen area with food, refrigerator run by a generator, and chairs, a tiny bed.

They ate and sat down to rest while Rachel climbed up to take a nap.

Somebody tried the radio and it worked, immediately filling the underground with the sonorous voice of Prince Hope. A plane roared overhead in the above ground world.

Like soldiers listening to Tokyo Rose just for something to do they sat in silence as Hope talked about them, about CRUSHER, about the need for democracy and human rights and an end to poverty.

"But that just can't happen while everyone has a gun and hundreds of CRUSHER rebels are loose to run wild on our streets," said Hope.

Way up top a truck roared, grinding gears, finally going away.

"We should just stay," said Korey.

"We'll find food, there's probly lots of food right here. We don't need to ever go back up there except for beer and cigarettes at night."

"I don't know," said Washington.

They sat, listening to Hope and giving it some serious thought.

Evey looked around. Not much room for Rachel to run. Maybe a good thing. But not much room to run, either.

"No," she said. "This won't work.

"We're going back. I thought it might, but it won't."

They had to wait for another big truck.

"We need to fight," Evey said.

"Fight?" said Korey.

"Are you kidding me? We'd be lucky as fuck ta stay alive or outa prison fer ten minutes. Fight?"

"I need to get back," said Washington.

"There's some things I need to do."

"Like what?" said Korey.

"Like live, man," said Washington.

"What's there to do here but dig? I ain't no gopher."

"Nope," said Korey.

"I think we need to continue with the vision of Reuben and Hector, see how far they got and continue digging and cover the whole thing and make a new country called Underground United States, the good ol' U.U.S.A.

"Whattaya think?

"And I thought you said we shouldn't kill anymore, Evey."

"I said fight," said Evey.

"I didn't say kill."

"How does that work?" said Korey.

"Well," said Evey, looking at Blake and also seeing Rachel now had one eye open.

"We've been talking about something. It's still kind of a secret."

"A secret," said Korey.

"Perfect.

"Sshhhhhh," he put a finger over his mouth and looked at Washington.

Washington didn't laugh. He just looked away at the sound of something farther on, down one of the dark tunnels.

Rachel scrunched her knees to her chest.

"I'm cold," she said.

Evey clicked off Prince Hope's voice in mid-sentence.

"We're going," she said.

"Now?" said Korey. "Right now?"

"We're staying," said Korey.

"Not me," said Washington.

Korey looked around, felt the cold wall, peeked around the corner at a long, dark hall.

"You sure?" said Evey.

"Yep," said Korey.

"I'm sure. I'm stayin'. I can do something with this."

He rubbed a palm over the jagged wall.

They shook hands, hugged, forked over anything in their pockets they thought Korey could use and then Korey walked them up to the front door.

And I pray, oh my god do I pray.
I pray every single day
For a revolution
— Four Non-Blondes, "What's Up?"

There was one exact moment, in fact, when I knew for sure that Al Gore would Never be President of the United States, no matter what the experts were saying — and that was when the whole Bush family suddenly appeared on TV and openly scoffed at the idea of Gore winning Florida. It was Nonsense, said the Candidate, Utter nonsense ... Anybody who believed Bush had lost Florida was a Fool.

The Media, all of them, were Liars & Dunces or treacherous whores trying to sabotage his victory ... Here was the whole bloody Family laughing & hooting & sneering at the dumbness of the whole world on National TV.

The old man was the real tip-off.

The leer on his face was almost frightening. It was like looking into the eyes of a tall hyena with a living sheep in its mouth. The sheep's fate was sealed, and so was Al Gore's.

— Hunter S. Thompson

EIGHT

He woke up on a Saturday morning, the morning unlike any other, with the sun out and the birds singing, when certain things are possible.

Billy got showered, dressed, brushed his teeth, happy in knowing what he was going to do with his Saturday. He walked into the hall and down the cement steps and approached the door.

In a moment he was outside and he almost didn't know how he got there it had happened so quickly because he had decided to just do it, not think it to death.

He was going for a walk. He looked back and up in a second or third floor window stood some of the staff, waving. He waved back and in his wave it said all that needed saying. Fuck you all.

Billy went right to it.

He found the place.

The place where he had met Shit-Fuck, Fuck-Shit, Motherfucker and the others.

In the grass he found a piece of something, a grey part of something. He picked it up and it was so light. He walked all around and, well, it had taken awhile to get here, and Saturday was not usually a day for long walks, but for sleeping until noon. He walked into the middle of the space to a circle or an oblong darkened area and it was warm there. He lay down, curled his knees to his chest with his hands for a pillow. He heard a meadowlark, smelled pig manure and drifted away.

He dreamed of home and then his dream down-shifted, turned left and he was again where he was, in the little patch like a pond in between trees and a cornfield. He was standing now. The Cornwall Boys, the little ones with the big feet and big heads, were talking to him, standing outside of their, well, spaceship.

Billy talked to the aliens, not even sure if it was the same ones as before. He talked out of his head and they talked out of theirs. They asked if he wanted to go for a ride and Billy, having been on a similar ride in a dream or not, not that long ago, and pretty sure he was dreaming now or not, said in his head, "sure, why not?"

Then they were all inside and some of them were at the controls and the screens and others showed Billy where to sit. He knew where to sit, but these ones must not have been along before, but they showed him to a comfortable cushion chair by a window. And they were in the air.

They saw it all, clouds, stars, mountains, rivers, oceans, animals, lots of people, lots of desert. Other round ships. They saw a face under a straw hat on many large screens and a little man playing in the dirt in the roses by a giant white house with lots of serious men in suits watching the man play.

They saw other stuff and some stuff they did not see because they went very fast most of the time though some of the time they just stayed in one spot almost still.

Billy opened his eyes and he felt the grass on his cheek and it was still warm.

He sat up because he had a decision to make.

He would either go back to the state mental hospital and his familiar bed and room and window or he would not.

Billy pulled his knees to his chin and he thought.

He got up and walked, through the trees, the bushes, back up the hill and to the little highway where he caught a ride and another and then he walked.

He stalked up to the front door and he did not knock because he knew the person was not home.

He pushed the front door and stepped inside.

Now he was.

He picked a newspaper from the floor and saw again, circled in pen, the letter to the editor that had got him installed in the Iowa state mental hospital.

He went to the little kitchen and found his favorite coffee cup on the table, with the Field of Dreams image. He poured the cold out in the sink and set to work to make fresh.

Billy sat at his kitchen table to wait for the coffee then went to his office, his little room where his home computer sat on the desk cluttered with books and coffee cups and looked straight out the beautiful window at the yard and the birds and the trees and the corn, his field of dreams of what is right and wrong and how it could be.

He sipped the coffee and went right to it writing again to his family and friends as if nothing had gone wrong, and in fact, perhaps nothing had.

Jeff,

Yes, both those biographies should be found at Amazon. THE LAST CAPTIVE is auto-biography, put together by A. C. Green. It is curious in several ways, its teller, Herman Lehmann, was a young German boy in Texas who did not then know English, when Apaches captured him. They were very hard on him while he was innately tough, just born fierce. He became one of them, early teens going on raids. Interesting to me how adept he became with bow & arrow, but kids can learn things quicker than adults usually will.

Then there was this feuding by and by inside their group, and his side were killed, and with his bow he killed his enemy before he could raise his rifle, and he fled, and lived alone a time. Then, it is interesting to me his ignorance of biology, and he tells some tall tales about wolves and rattlesnakes, which sounds like white man superstition.

Example, he portrays wolves to be too stupid, too stupid to survive thousands of years taking down large prey. By then he has been with the whites, learned English and crap. Oh, too, if I am correct, Quanah Parker last Comanche chief had adopted him. CAPTIVE I did read twice, am now rereading EMPIRE OF THE SUMMER MOON. There are photos in both books, both books have this one of Cynthia Ann Parker, back with whites, nursing her child, fear and mistrust and tragedy in her eyes, as she had gone completely native, then all the time attempting to escape, return to the Comanches. The child in her arms, Prairie Flower, did become as a little girl very popular among her white relatives, then died, and soon Cynthia Ann died.

Cynthia Ann raised with Comanches had also been very

tough, combative, had become accepted. She was physically quite large for those times, and her son, Quanah, was thus large. Comanches were originally a mountain people, short with stocky legs, maybe that is best for horse back. Best cavalry in known history. There is much of that in SUMMER MOON.

So your uncle had property in Bigfoot country. Probably he knew it, or, had been told. Yeah, it is rough turning properties loose. Well, my sister and I keep this place to a stalemate. I have to just go with the surf. With my own stuff, a big wooden trunk full of manuscripts, a chest of drawers, more LL manuscripts, I imagine a miracle, something, to stop it, damn. Medicine Dog is buried here. Our parents both passed here, in this "Gallery" of Lyla's. What a family. Mike and Bonnie feel all the time they must tell they do not believe in Spirit. And Bonnie and I will not let this place turn to some money.

Further,
Bill

Geoffrey,

Hi. Wow, surprised how I warped a sentence. "The grade school kiddies in Woodsville do not allow unsupervised children wrestling on their grounds." How did I not catch that one.

The dipshit grade school authorities in Woodsville do not allow unsupervised children wrestling on their grounds. The grade school kiddies in Woodsville are not allowed to wrestle unsupervised on the school grounds.

I have written, maybe not in these Postings but in LL, in my fifteenth year back when hospitals were affordable by poor people I was hospitalized with asthma several times, in Aransas Pass and in Corpus Christi. They would stabilize me with injections and/or oxygen, then I would there lie for a couple days, I forget but any case I read by somebody THE FLYING SAUCERS ARE REAL, this paperback, which previously had been in the popular men's magazine, True Magazine. All this is - probably it can be found at Amazon Books, you know - is historical accounts of space ships viewed, going back before biblical inclusive. Ships hovering over cities and so on. Thought I: Why finish high school, hell, why even learn to drive a car. Being of superior intelligence I should find out about all this, meet these other beings. This was one year before meeting Ray Stanford who talked for us at the Lion's Club in Aransas, being RD Hatch III's father was head of the Lion's Club. I think 8 of we believers, including Packy I think, though then he did not believe, got out of school for this. At the Grill Café. Uh, to say, there the story was the UFO beings are indeed human anyway.

So, in the hospital, late 1955, I had looked at HS, and noted I had learned nothing. Not since maybe the fourth grade. There was nothing there.

Oh, I had taken in Spanish words, if or not I failed Spanish 1, probably had. English I was perfect in pre HS, I would discover taking aptitude tests from psychiatrist or psychologists in Houston via my worried mother, 1956 Don't need to remember no stinking English grammar terminology, I know what a sentence is.

Well, I had to be arrogant. I did keep alive. I did enter Pan American college. Feh. Had taken a GED.

I was very hard on my parents. Crazed, manic depressed, gone Beat. Am saying, am a seer. I will talk to Madrea. We have been something, Amerindians, something. The US Empire is going over a cliff.

We shall see. Seems I hurt my knee badly using my new ax in Aransas before coming here, but glad to have some steel, but my age does not really impress me and I'll see my grandkids getting along, GED tests or never.

Couple nights back Kelly and Janus had old friends Vivian and Gary over. You know, they have about 3 daughters, and oldest is Amanda who as very little girls knew Madrea. Amanda is still not married, makes good money as a bartender.

I try to keep to Olive family taboo-speak now. I don't do it well. We were not even drinking much. Or not with Bill. But, Gary is very nice, sociable. I began to slip up. It was too hard for him, soon he was trying to stop me, telling me he is just here to see old friends he loves, he was desperately even telling me that he agrees with me, but this has to be for some other time etc. I did get hold of myself.

SO! As one drunken lout friend used to say. IT HAS COME TO THIS!

Further,

Bill

Man. Who is he. Where is he. Why is he here. Isolated in space on a round mass of matter live some several billion intelligent beings, man. But what is his origin. Some say he evolved from the slime of the sea. Others that a god created an Adam and Eve and he was their descendent. Yet others speculate that he was brought here sometime in the distant past and that the earth was colonized by men from another dying planet, yet despite the theories and explanations, the answer remains an unsolved mystery. As to where he is, that's easier, a planet 8,000 miles in diameter, located in a remote portion of a galaxy, somewhere in infinite space. Why is he here? That, too remains an unsolved mystery. Occupied by his daily affairs, he finds little time to contemplate, that question, except for those moments, on a clear night, when man pauses and looks to the star-filled heavens, and in his mind stirs an unanswered question.

— Rod Serling

NINE

The Pres'dent.

Sat on his rocking horse with blue stars. A stick horse, a red one, lay wide-eyed on the floor.

He watched the man on the screen as he rocked, now stopped rocking, feet dangling, not quite touching the shined hardwood floor, as bright and polished as the main corridor connecting Unit One & Unit Two inside the Federal Supermax Penitentiary in Florence, Colorado, the hard marble the pride of a prisoner who shined it every morning.

The Pres'dent placed a finger on his chin and listened. He did not get most of the jokes, any of them. He saw the shooting and the dying and the crying that followed the talking by the man in the hat on the big screen and he cooed and got a bubble and needed to be burped.

The Pres'dent nodded to the man in the suit and was immediately changed into his Leader costume, blue cape, red tights, white stars, white booties, red mask.

He smiled and giggled because he liked to wear the suit.

If truth be known, Americans are no more free than were Germans under Gestapo Germany. "Freedom and Democracy America" is the greatest lie in the world.

Countries sink into tyranny easily. Those born today don't know the freedom of the past and are unaware of what has been taken away.

— Paul Craig Roberts

TEN

Mike!

Hey, thanks for some clarification. Sure, and I did sign it. Don't know exactly why Kelly did not give me an explanation. It has been thus, we talk in sound bites. This I do say to Kelly, goddamn sound bites. He is distracted someway.

Sorry you have allergy trouble. As said, Bonnie came into it, few decades back some point. Good none of you are gone asthmatic. Well, yes, I dodge that, so should be excused for my means. Maybe I would use all these means without any asthma background. Nothing is sacred but humor. Man does not live by bread alone. All work and no play makes Jack a dull boy. White man plumb crazy. Give me a beer. A weak man walks on three legs. A wise man breaks his apple.

Really am enjoying this A PEOPLE'S HISTORY OF THE UNITED STATES, by Howard Zinn. It is online at history-isaweapon.com with typos, just slammed in. History is a Weapon says to the reader, tell us what typos. I am right up against World War II. There has been all this labor warfare with capitalism from later 1800s to Second World War. Bloody shit. Cops are mad dogs, will hit anything moving, shoot in bloodlust. The troops nearly the same, they are brought in. The glutton billionaires at top are dull, saps who cause national depressions, etcetera.

I am curious how noble Zinn will handle the "Holocaust" of world War II. The atom bombing of Japan and so forth. He was alive up till 911, possibly he is still alive....He did know of my author friend, Mike Novak, gave him a blurb of applause, on some of the Truther paperbacks Novak has sent me.

The facts, and Zinn starts with Columbus, are ugly, horrific. "American Exceptionality" is a bloody fart. Oh well.

This history is a page turner. A person who takes a peep ought to well read on. I had heard of it but had not sensed it is this great.

Nasal agitations can be diverted, sometimes. Stimulants, depressants. Heroin would help. Its opposite, cocaine, would.

Aware you would not mess with maligned drugs, I but point out, it is the distraction....Because it is nervous reaction from one's confused biology/psychology. Thus, violent exercise, drunkenness, these things can toss it off temporarily. As in hick-ups one holds one's breath and counts to sixty. And, everybody is different....I advocate psychedelics...,.Wherein one cares not one has a runny nose. Is my point.... Vitamin C is good.

Further Out, Bill

***

Caryl,

Thank you for photos. What state is Lago Vista in? The river here, the Medina, has gone back down very much, re. mail to Geoffrey yesterday. Now we want rain, the grass is too dry.

We are in this tremendous influx of fire ants. Second morning before coffee in a row I put on soiled jean cutoffs I am attacked. They like sweat. I had tried to hang last night's fresher shorts from the belt, but they ambushed me again anyway, though not nearly so bad as yesterday before coffee. I took like a hundred bites to my legs and privates yesterday, maybe two hundred, very annoying.

You know, I'm just running around here like a Comanche at rest, but must figure how to do this. Put my used shorts in a drawer maybe.... Maybe not....I need to get in to purchase more Off from the rip-off grocery store - this works best, though my daughter dislikes its chemicals, she was using organic stuff which is much slower....Off kills these tiny maniacs besides, really does turn them back....

I'd said, I had known nothing of the military's using private property for their activities in the past. I have only heard of this with the Jade Helm business. But like they were hollering in Bastrop, the government has more property to practice on than does anyone.

And, I understand, this is a larger scale, huge scale, enormous.

People such as Kelly & Janus who only watch government

controlled news are still working at believing there is nothing new going on. But, I was a bit surprised to encounter young folks in the Ivanhoe area who know of and wonder about Jade Helm, who are not really readers of anything.

It must be coming originally from the Web, though it has become word of mouth, and a person might still believe the 911 official cartoon (plane enters building like it is a mirage, a veritable cartoon) (First reels of this on TV had the nose of passenger jet sticking out the other side of skyscraper, before red explosion, but "they" got nervous with that much, took out that part - it is still available, on the Web), yet be worried about Jade Helm, wonder why is it on the common news stations this information is so shallow. "Believers" of 911 account are nervous why no more information about this Jade Helm stuff....Yes, you are right. People have less trust, even Democrats now have less trust.

Nothing of past US history is as fantastic as post 911. War is horror, and worse in modern war, but the warfare post 911 has more young US fellows killing themselves, way more, much more than are killed in these ugliest ever military actions.

Before Larry King retired, I saw his friend, Willie Nelson, and next his friend, Jesse Ventura, speak boldly about 911. How strange - to speak at all is bold. Ventura did say: Why can't we talk about it!... Fucking nuts - that is already years ago....

Well, old friend, you have heard about author George Orwell's 1984. And we are far, far beyond any 1984. Wild Bill Blackbird does not exaggerate. We are far, far beyond.

Mike Blackbird was yesterday telling me of this book he had not got around to. He could not recall title and author, he was trying. I never did discover WHY had he thought to read this novel, but in his mutterings I did catch on. Mike, 1984, George Orwell! Yes, Mike! It is more popular than ever before!

What siblings have I. All this real life with Billy Frank could never sell as fiction. Fucking nuts.

I am always glad to hear from you, Caryl.

love, Billy

Tyranny was brought to Americans intentionally by their government. Perhaps it began in 1992 with the unaccountable use of police power against an American family at Ruby Ridge. Randy Weaver's 12-or 13-year-old son was shot in the back and murdered by federal marshals.

Then his wife was murdered with a shot through her throat while she stood at the door of her home holding a baby in her arms. There was no justification for this gratuitous violence against a peaceful American family, and the federal marshals who murdered were not held accountable.

The Congress, "the people's representatives" held a hearing, and those responsible for murdering a family told the representatives that they had "to trust the police".

A year later, 1993, the Clinton regime murdered, using poison gas as well as gun fire, more than 100 members of the Branch Davidian religious sect in Waco, Texas.

Women and children comprised most of the victims of "freedom and democracy America." The Branch Davidians had done nothing except be different.

— Paul Craig Roberts

ELEVEN

Prince Hope sat at his desk in his new office in the high-rise building in Minneapolis on the same floor as Mike Braxton's F.B.I. office down the hall.

He looked out the one window straight into the limestone Foshay Tower.

Hope wrote on a yellow legal pad.

"Head right, mind right, brain freeze, rite, right, write ... site, sight, cite, might, white, go team go, fight, fight, fight."

The radio played banjo music laced with harmonica ... wait for it, wait for it ... Good God Y'all! Hooh! And then the Big Really Red Chevy commercial.

He slid his chair over the floor to the window and looked down. He could almost see some people.

He propelled himself back to his desk where his computer sat next to his legal pad with the nonsense words, opened the little drawer that he had never opened before, found some black electrical tape, tore off, bit off an end and the person on the other end, looking through the little window on Hope's computer screen saw Hope's face in close-up and his fingers fumbling with the tape and then nothing.

Black.

Imagine really black and that's it.

Our problem is civil obedience. Our problem is the numbers of people all over the world who have obeyed the dictates of the leaders of their government and have gone to war, and millions have been killed because of this obedience... Our problem is that people are obedient all over the world, in the face of poverty and starvation and stupidity, and war and cruelty. Our problem is that people are obedient while the jails are full of petty thieves, and all the while the grand thieves are running the country. That's our problem... people are obedient, all these herdlike people.

— Howard Zinn

TWELVE

Hi Billy: so good to hear from you. Sounds as if all are enjoying the river. I sure would. That was a crazy rainy spring. My daughter lives in Lago Vista where the Colorado is swollen about a block or two from her condo. It could a lot more water.

You know, I was thinking about the army using private property all thru the years: the terrain. was rugged, rocky out in hot west Texas, and a big factor with the ranchers was that we used to trust out government. No longer is that the case... our government is our enemy. Perhaps that is the heart of all the chaos . The gov lies so no matter what they say, the people are not calmed or trusting. Gotta go fix supper. Love, Caryl

To: Geoffrey
'He then represented the King family in a wrongful death civil trial, King family vs. Loyd Jowers and "other unknown conspirators." During a trial that lasted four weeks Bill produced over seventy witnesses. Jowers, testifying by deposition, stated that James Earl Ray was a scapegoat, and not involved in the assassination. Jowers testified that Memphis police officer Earl Clark fired the fatal shots. On December 8, 1999, the Memphis jury found Jowers responsible and found that the assassination plot included also "governmental agencies." The jury took less than an hour to find in favor of the King family for the requested sum of $100.'

Geoffrey, this above is from William Pepper.com. It is what I had spoken of, googled via william pepper / mlk / fbi.
I was not talking about "efforts to prove the innocence of James Earl Ray," though that was done, in 1999. What I was talking about, this 1999 civil suit was not allowed in the regular news. I am talking about police state. International police state. What citizens have even known the King family is angry with the government for killing MLK ?

72

AND I SUPPOSE WE DIDN'T GO TO THE MOON EITHER is next read, is on this table. I have been a bit slow with THE BROTHERS KARAMOZOV, which is relative, philosophically relative, genius work of fiction, in Western Civilization. What people in the 1800s were saying in Russia.

I understand, most citizens are less interested than am I and some others, Truthers. CIA and ilk felt gonzo after easily taking out JFK, MLK. So they did 911. They are more stressed from that one, have gained nothing yet but fear. They are rabid, best to watch them.

Grocery stores have these cheapest plastic bottles for fruit juices, with screw on tops. What I had a cork in was a glass wine bottle. What I had been instructed to use is piece of paper towel folded over plastic neck and tied, loosely, Madrea thinks more to keep out bugs. A cork could have had a plastic jug to blast apart, as is I retained at least 2 thirds of those contents of the wine bottle. I applied correct paper top to it too next.

Love,
Bill

Bill,
I hadn't heard of this method for making wine. I'll look it up. So, it was in a plastic jug of juice with a cork? I haven't seen juice come like this, but yeah, in retrospect, a cork would not allow breathing.

The exploding cork incident could be a scene from Suttree, my favorite Cormac McCarthy book, which focuses on a colorful cast of dwellers along the river in Knoxville, Tennessee in the early '50s, making their own alcohol and getting by. So, how does the wine taste? I guess the taste varies depending on the kind of fruit juice used etc.?

In the high 90s here, very humid, low 90s at night. We run the AC for a bit when we get too worn down.

Well, better get to some other mail before the others awaken. I enjoyed your wine making story. I did skim some a couple internet pages about Pepper's efforts to prove the innocence of James Earl Ray. Will read more by and by.

Love, Geof

Mike,

Just now have googled Lee Berger and Homo Naledi. Too much for me to read there, loads of scull parts, bone pieces. Will wait to hear further. Thank you for telling me.

On possible existing Neanderthal - a Russian anthropologist says why not of a type furtive in mountain reaches of Pakistan.

Neanderthal is not large, burly but under six feet. Perhaps in the US forests there are a couple of hominid species, the Sasquatch type has males big as largest Kodiak bears, we hear, but the southern sort is still 2 or 3 times larger than a Neanderthal, if an adult. Juveniles get seen. Witnesses get stunned at the size of an adult. When it amuses one to be seen.

Too bad, these woods here would only do for a Neanderthal size ninja. But the Big Thicket works out fine. Probably, my pollen allergies are better for me here.

Good morning, feels like it is less than seventy degrees, before sun up. For looking Nordic, I am thin blooded.

Looked then at lee berger/homo naledi again and there are a bunch of places to check, some having more commentary. A clamor, hungry egos. Nice human looking picture from National Geographic, someone you could have a talk with.

I had been a bit distracted besides preoccupied when your email came in yesterday. I had begun answering yours, also sipping more wine. Need to spare my wine. Anyway....took a time before I got back for a second listening of #95 of Jim Kessler's The Real Deal. These go two hours and most people I know don't have that patience. I wonder why. The title of Jim Kessler's The Real Deal #95 is James McCanney On Planets, Comets, and the Electric Universe. There is new stuff there, too, Mike. Had you known comets are not made of ice?

I had not known this. That the planets of our solar system were originally comets?

I will take James M.'s word for all this. These are videos and you can see this man is absolutely un-self conscious and unpretentious. This cat is interested. Same with Kessler.

Ah, it is eight o'clock and the animals wish to scurry. I should add this: On second listen to #95 last evening I remembered it is not either quite devoid of "politics." There is notice the CIA controls NASA. Besides, they want no talk of extraterrestrials and they want control of all talk of extraterrestrials. Oh well.

Further Out,
Bill

QUOTE REMOVED BY ORDER OF DHS, UNITED STATES
DEPARTMENT OF HOMELAND SECURITY. [DHS US2FA]

When the Branch Davidian compound was attacked by a tank spewing chemical warfare and then burnt to the ground, insouciant Americans were told that justice had been done to child abusers. No one objected that the same "justice" had also been done to the allegedly abused children.

Again the "representatives of the people" held a hearing.

The result was that the Clinton criminal regime and Janet Reno got approval for dealing effectively with those who violate gun laws.

Ruby Ridge and Waco established the precedents that the US government could murder large numbers of Americans, and at Waco some foreigners, without consequence.

The "representatives of the people" accepted the executive branch's lies in order to avoid having to hold the executive branch accountable for what were clearly without any doubt capital crimes against American citizens for which the federal perpetrators of these crimes should have been tried and executed.

— Paul Craig Roberts

THIRTEEN

Korey stalked deeper into The Underground Kingdom of Reuben and Hector, following their FuckYoo signposts on the walls that were either to each other or to someone who might follow them. Maybe they thought they were writing in Vietnamese. At some intersections someone had taken great effort to pound a stake into the hard floor and tack up little bits of board that said how many miles and which direction to Lake Wobegon, Bumfuck, Iowa, to Mayfield, to Mayberry, to Oz, to Hollywood.

He saw also drawings of flying saucers, Bigfoots, dinosaurs, sabertooth tigers. Some of the drawings looked old and not quite what Reuben and Hector would have come up with, but so hard to really tell.

He kept going, down around, sometimes up, sometimes down, until he came to the end of the wired caverns with the low-light electricity. He had found lots of stuff, supplies left by the others, lots of Seven Dwarfs stuff like picks, shovels, headlamps. Also beer cans, pop cans, wrappers, apple cores. He tried to clean up as he went.

He shined his heavy duty flashlight down this way and that, the final "Y" where Reuben and Hector had probably stopped. Something caught his eye and he approached it cautiously.

He thought maybe this is just as far as they got because they ran out of time or they chose not to go any farther, for some reason.

Korey heard sounds, digging? chirping? tweets? cave birds? *Ooooh*. He felt a breeze and smelled something that said don't go any farther.

Mice, probably, he thought, pushing the thought of giant juicy rats to the back of his head.

Something buzzed him and he hit the deck where he found himself right by the symbol etched in the wall, an X with an arrow through the middle pointing down the dark way.

He pushed himself up and shined the flashlight hard,

down in the direction of the right-hand corridor, keeping one hand on a wall.

What *is* that? he wondered.

What the ... hell?

OHHH.

OHHHH my fucking goddamn shit.

OOHH God. Oh God.

OH, Jesus.

Oh Man.

Korey had come to the end of the dark corridor, into a little room.

He ducked to enter.

He shined the light all around.

In the little room was an area set off, by a white picket fence. There was a mound and on the mound was a drawing inside a frame of a horse wearing an alien blanket with three fingers on each hand and three toes on each foot. There was one half of the treasure map of Reuben and Hector and other stuff scattered around and on top of the mound.

Korey opened the little gate and set foot inside the fenced shrine.

He found bones scattered around, and a black and white photo of the real, the first Geronimo, three bullet casings, a Star Wars Wookie Happy Meal toy that Korey recalled when that actually came out, a Stratego Spy piece, wooden, some sticks were laid out in weird formations, triangles, the Pi sign, an X.

What the heck, thought Korey. He couldn't bring himself to swear in this place, it didn't seem right.

He knelt down and saw written on this side of the picket fence:

I left in love, in laughter, and in truth. — Bill Hiks.

And as he knelt and looked over the top of the fencing he saw a Lego toy on the cave floor, sort of a robin's-egg blue little car. He went over to it, picked it up. Inside were three figures, two men and a woman, blonde.

QUOTE REMOVED BY ORDER OF DHS, UNITED STATES
DEPARTMENT OF HOMELAND SECURITY. [DHS US2FA]

We own the whole world, or we think we do. And yet we own very little of it. We can't manage it. It's too big. We don't know all that's out there.

— M.K. Davis

FOURTEEN

Mike,

Hope you and Wendy are having a good trip.

I have just read something you would enjoy. I was enjoying it, wanting it to not end.

Preliminary Report of the 1999 Six Rivers National Forest Expedition

by J. Richard Greenwell, Expedition Leader

I checked and the above is all you need, if or whenever you might feel like looking at it. I had in boredom tonight gone back to Bigfoot Encounters, to the more interesting section, Biology, Scientific Papers & Field Reports. Greenwell I had not heard of, his is the last one. It is hard for me to find anything new there, sometimes lately I have reread something, as was with the Jordi Magraner paper. Greenwell has passed, born in 1942 only made it to 2005. He is likeable, a bit funny and surly, but even more cautious than Magraner. He refuses to conclude anything from the 1999 trip. But it is a good story, in this wilderness I had not heard of, in northern California, a fabulous place, the Siskiyou Wilderness. Reading it, I noticed the different ways you would enjoy this one.

Hatch called today, we hadn't talked in a while. He told me the story he had told you, guy in was it HEB parking lot who had seen his Democrat bumper sticker and he acted conversational but then abruptly is offensive and stupid, pissed off Richard, who instantly exploded with profanity and the guy dug out, speeded away. So Hatch says he is too old for fistfights but he is still infuriated.

Further,

Bill

Yo, Bill:

I never read that magazine, Argosy, very much. Didn't see that piece.

Well, getting DNA from the group, looks like it will be hard. I still
can't get hold of Jordi Magraner's original witness reports. I need
to closely examine those reports. If you figure out how to find them,
let me know. At this point, as far as I can see, that's the only decent evidence around.
I'm going with Wendy to her cabin in the mountains. No internet
there. Be gone for a couple days or so. Check you later.

Mike

QUOTE REMOVED BY ORDER OF DHS, UNITED STATES
DEPARTMENT OF HOMELAND SECURITY. [DHS US2FA]

9/11 clearly, without any doubt, destroyed American liberty. Even if you are so brainwashed as to believe an obviously false story of the event, even if you believe that a few Saudi Arabians without government or intelligence service support outwitted all 16 US intelligence agencies, the National Security Council, all intelligence agencies of Washington's vassals abroad, outwitted Israel's Mossad, US Air Traffic Control, caused US Airport Security to fail four times in one hour on the same day, and prevented for the first time in history the US Air Force from sending fighters to intercept off course airliners, the fact remains the same: the US government used 9/11 to destroy the constitutional protections of US liberty.

The raw, ugly, but true fact that "our" government has destroyed American liberty is the reason that every one of us is subject to experiencing the abuses that John Whitehead describes.

Who will be next? You? Me? Your Wife? Your Son? Your daughter? Your aged and infirm parents?

When it happens, it was the American people who permitted it.

— Paul Craig Roberts

FIFTEEN

Korey found Washington sitting. He sat next to him.

They sat right in the big city cavern surrounded by big buildings and busy people going left and right, lots of vehicle sounds, cars, buses, a light rail train over about two blocks. Some clouds filtered the bright sun. If they would have looked up they would have seen a couple of airliners headed into or out of Bloomington. They didn't.

Hey.

Hey.

I found something!

What?

I don't know!

We need to go back there.

Why?

I'm not sure, wanna go?

Sure, yeah.

"It's The Woo," said Korey as they stood by the little white picket fence at the end of the cave passages.

"The Woo."

"Yeah, The Woo. It's what runs everything."

"Thought it was batteries."

"Nope, The Woo. Spirits."

"Spirits? I doubt it."

"Not really Spirits."

"You just said. Spirits."

"Yeah, but.

"Like when you die, or almost die, you see things, things you don't see now."

"Oh, okay.

"Now I get it.

"Not."

"You are such a stupid fuck."

"Then why did you bring me here?"

"I don't know.

"I thought you would think it's cool."
"It is cool. I didn't say that."
"Oh, I thought …"
"No, no, it's cool, man.
"It's cool."

QUOTE REMOVED BY ORDER OF DHS, UNITED STATES
DEPARTMENT OF HOMELAND SECURITY. [DHS US2FA]

When it was decided to make the movie about his life called *Serpico*, Al Pacino invited Serpico to stay with him at a house that Pacino had rented in Montauk, New York.
When Pacino asked why he had stepped forward, Serpico replied, "Well, Al, I don't know. I guess I would have to say it would be because ... if I didn't, who would I be when I listened to a piece of music?"
— Frank Serpico

A man once said that the pinnacle of success is when you've finally lost interest, in money, compliments, and publicity.
— Todd Snider

SIXTEEN

Steve,

Kat and Choyota wanted me to get up, see the dawn. I have not had a "good" life, have had an interesting life, inside boredom, disgust, revulsion, heartbreak.

I haven't seen any red dawns. Nor red suns, which McCarthy has throughout his fiction. McCarthy's books have good writings but he peaked early, or is he alive? Was not there this plain crap fiction about a US submarine called RED DAWN? It sold, became a movie. Murray R. who has zero good sense of books wanted his name in TG, got it at the last, then he would never read TG, but when I was looking after his blind father he told me how wonderful is RED DAWN and I must read it. Gawd, might be I ingested a page.

What happens to people.

Yesterday I went in with Kelly quickly, needed eggs, more juice for recreation, he needed cattle cubes and hay. Another week we do a bigger trip and I post a hundred to Madrea who is doing ok, is on the substitute teacher list but yet to get going there. I think it is tomorrow night late Kelly and Janus bring in Jessica and Jake.

I don't know for how long. I see Kelly, not every day, and we get along and mostly I dodge Blackbird Taboo-Speak. Yes, we are a little mad out here. Why are we in Vietnam? Oh, we got out, got whipped, and the Merchants of War did fine. Uh, why are we in Syria, uh, we are getting whipped now, we will be gone and the Merchants of War do well always. Kelly and I were getting along yesterday, talked about arthritis. I took it into Crop Circles, tried to sum it to Kelly at this point, as this does not ruffle him, hell, it should not.

Oh, I mentioned how I had recommended Crop Circles to Caryl, better if she would not worry about Muslims and fake refugees who are Muslims, and Kelly supposed she likes Donald Trump. I said I don't know, maybe she does. He declared she probably does.

He went on a bit about the current situation of Republicans/

Democrats. He wishes I would believe the Democrats are better. He never says so. I know he wishes I would concede a bit. I said, hell, Kelly, they are all the same, Republicans/Democrats, they are all liars.

Ah, possibly Bernie is not a liar, I said. In same breath he chuckled that I said maybe Bernie is not a liar, Kelly raised voice that I had been doing pretty good today then when I talk like this he wants to crash the truck into these trees. We are mad out here but with Kelly if I just stop speaking we automatically are "getting along" again.

The Republicans had Ron Paul, the Democrats had Dennis Kuscinage (sp). They were got rid of. Democrats and Republicans is one farce. Republicans act more surly, Democrats more kindly, and they work hand in hand. Kelly loves Obama's style, and he now does not notice his lies. This is confounding. Kelly had become a trouble maker while still a co-captain of the NMSU football team. I was there toward end of his last year and he and I attended a Vietnam demonstration on the campus and we psyched out a large group of these "cowboys," redneck USNM students who chewed tobacco. Hippies were expected to not be physical, and we scared these young chumps, big mob of them who wanted to disrupt the demonstration.

We did not allow them to. How this is done, take one and hold his eyes, he freezes. Do same to another. Kelly would later laugh to Janus how Bill was getting crazy, maybe so, can't exactly recall now. Soon Kelly got drafted, and journalists were interested in him, NMSU radical leader gets hair cut in boot camp, photographed. We have not talked about all this in a long time. Can old age just kill logic? People who have had to go along, or they thought, just forget? Old age just depresses people? No more free spirit? No free thoughts? So what Crop Circles.

Bill never had anything to lose anyway. Hell no.

Getting a flock of wild turkeys outside this window now, across the fence the clearing, pasture. I could hit one first shot with a .22, rifle. Should we not have guns or ammunition all this will be hard enough. Wild turkey is about as good as it gets, maybe good as venison. Ah. Maybe. Naa.

Here I am, untaught. But when I can get hemp oil with the THC still in, I will take out my arthritis. Do that and my age will not count. Argh.

Yeah, this is a STRANGE TIME. When I am again reading the available relit hominid information off the USA Net, I have this sentiment, information. I care much.

Guess I'll have a third cup and maybe take a shower at Bonnie's, as this plumbing has roots or rats or no telling.

Further,

Bill

Mike,

Glad to hear you checked out Jordi Magraner. Since telling you of his famous paper on the relict (I forget why some say "relict" and some "relic") hominid, I found that he was surprisingly young when killed, 35, not Russian (forget how I thought that, though Russians are often involved now), but Spaniard, who had previously been living in France. Quite a mysterious figure, something of an adventurer, he and a servant boy were murdered in 2002 in Pakistan at a house he rented, he had some powerful watchdogs who were drugged during the murder, and the authorities sounded hostile to him, figured he had nefarious activity.

Well, gee, he was rather brilliant, very scientific (a zoologist), and handled English well enough though I could not find all of his big words, mostly on anatomy, but one was "survivance," for "survival," which also is not in this large dictionary you gave me. What a remarkable individual, rather romantic actually....Terrible he got killed so early.

Already some years back, originally I had encountered his paper through "Bigfoot Encounters," and had just lately thought to go back and look through his paper again. The site had been run by an organized woman, who died shortly after I had begun looking about in it, and, it stays there, but seems to never have anything new since her death. There is though piles of stuff there, poorer and decent enough. Now to get Magraner's paper you can simply google Jordi Magraner. His work has been for me perhaps the most interesting found there, though probably there is where I first heard of Zana. There is more of these or this hominid, like Zana, for example with another woman I think who has passed, her name slips me and it will be a task locating it again, but this very reasonable woman who could get along with the natives - I forget what country but Euro-Asian somewhere - had with native help observed these beings from some distance. I should have written down the woman's name, when I did again have it several days ago - forget how I lately found her again. Heh, maybe I'll get to her again. But, this sounds like same type, like Zana. Human, naked and very hairy but a species, ancient, quite furtive.

Well, it is raining, been raining slowly but steadily all night. Not in San Antonio, as I hear news in the night off the classical station, only cloudy in San Antonio. Nice to have rain, but it tosses off the dog walk.

Further,

Bill

QUOTE REMOVED BY ORDER OF DHS, UNITED STATES
DEPARTMENT OF HOMELAND SECURITY. [DHS US2FA]

The Spirit World ripples and weaves all through our world. The Mountain Apus has a Spirit, the trees Standing Ones that grow on that mountain, have a Spirit, and the Masters of Hide and Seek have woven their world in between the two. You can see it when you walk and feel of their realms. It is not woo, but a Sacred and Holy way of walking upon our Mother Earth. Pima Ta Taka Nee, WE ARE ALL RELATED. Wado Thank you for sharing very nice.
Xo

— (Snow Walker Prime YouTube Channel comments section)

SEVENTEEN

Actually and Charlie Googled, "how to scare the American people into not being stupid."

"Fake an alien invasion. War Of The Worlds.

"But still stupid, is what it says," said Charlie.

"Hmm," said Actually as the rest gathered around the table to begin the warm-up for the show.

"This is Moltvik, a real journalist from the half planet Sht-up on the other side of The Moon, reporting on assignment from Hollywood Earth."

"It's just a ride."

"Documents have been released to the group CRUSH-LEEKZ."

"It's the end of the world, yes, as we know it."

"And I feel fine," said Charlie.

"Yes, well," said Actually.

"How are we going to fight the repression this way"?

"Hmm, yes. Hmmm."

"Can you please quit saying hmmm."

"Yes."

"And now ...

"Are we on?

"... And now ... we join ... in progress ... another episode of "The Americans."

"The Americans" is brought to us each week by Razor Wire Dental Floss, it's good for you.

Also by Crisis Actors Of The Homeland, Operation Mockingbird, Operation Northwoods, COINTELPRO, and by Craft and Blackwater, bringing you the Boston bombing, Sandy Hook, San Bernardino and so much more.

And now, "The Americans," ...

It's true that the newcomers to Washington, D.C. are different than ever before ... but after all is said and done ... they are Americans.

We return to our story.

We find Skippy The Construction Worker sitting on his ass on a stack of concrete blocks.

Skippy is a tender for the brick and block layers working to build the wall around the Washington, D.C. Beltway ... to separate The White House, the FBI, the CIA, the Pentagon, the Congress and the Washington Press Corps from normal human beings.

Skippy already has the mud ready, the scaffolding ready, all the mud boards ready and primed and stocked.

He's on break, smoking a cigarette, waiting for the brick and block layers to show up to begin work.

He sees the Mad Dog being taken into the White House on a heavy chain, the oil to be poured into the rivers, the chainsaws, the protester cages, the tanks for the police, the lap dogs, the false documents, everything that will be needed for the next four years.

Finally, the other workers begin to arrive. They park their trucks, haul out their tools, say their hellos and get to work building the wall around the Washington, D.C. Beltway ... to separate The White House, the FBI, the CIA, the Pentagon, the Congress and the Washington Press Corps from normal human beings.

Scattered around the job site are the wooden boards to be tacked up all around the new wall with the message:

"Let me put it this way: while 9/11 was a US "deep state" operation (probably subcontracted for execution to the Israelis), the entire Washington "swamp" has been since "9/11 accomplice after the fact" by helping to maintain the cover-up. If this is brought into light, then thousands of political careers are going to crash and burn into the scandal."

We now hear again from the most dangerous blogger in the universe — Mark, in his parents' basement.

Mark is working on his latest vlog. He has decided to switch from blogging to vlogging, so now his stuff is available on YouTube and the world can finally see the face of Mark.

In order to disguise himself so that he can still go to Too Much Food for milk without being mobbed for autographs Mark sits with his back to his computer and we see Mark in a mirror on the wall, which Mark says will mean that those who see him in public will not recognize him because his face will be totally opposite.

We continue.

Mark's Vlog:

"Moon Dust & Cheetos Dust Are Both Orange. Coincidence?"

In the Parallelogram Office we find Pres'dent Cosmo Nutt at his Big Desk drawing on his big yellow legal pad ... working on some last-minute dollar signs, boobs and tanks before he must go down to The Camo Ball.

In The Big Hall ... we find all the guests dancing around a cherry tree decorated with copies of The 9/11 Commission Report and The Warren Commission Report ... in a conga line ... and bowing to the cherry tree ... to the beat of the band ... The Good Americans ...

... to be followed at midnight by the Baby Boomer Rap Group ... Rage Against The Mu-ja-ha-deen.

The party guests drink camo wine, all dressed in formal camo, circle the cherry tree, turning to bow at the chorus, to the beat of The Good Americans new hit song ...

"Dance Like An American ..."

Lets listen in to the lyrics of "Dance Like An American ..."

... Oh way oh, oh way oh ... way oh, way ohhhh ...

Dance Like An American ... ... Dance Like An American ...

... Put the Bop in the bop she bop she bop

... Put the ram in the ramma lamma ding dong.

Ding dong.

Meanwhile ... we now find ...

Skippy the construction worker YouTube self-taught demolition expert singing karaoke at the Paul Wellstone/Hale Boggs Crash Landing Bar across the river:

Thinkin' 'bout burnin' it down boys .
nothin's ever gonna be the same in this town,
thinkin' 'bout burnin' it down.

QUOTE REMOVED BY ORDER OF DHS, UNITED STATES
DEPARTMENT OF HOMELAND SECURITY. [DHS US2FA]

Anyone who challenges the prevailing orthodoxy
finds himself silenced with surprising effectiveness.
— George Orwell

… by the time the public demands an enquiry, the
perpetrators will be dead.
Do we hang their children?
— from the comments section

EIGHTEEN

M_{ike,}

I was saving the above for a letter to Geoffrey tomorrow. Planned to get a little drunk and wail a little. See, I am laughing, I think I am funny. However, Geoffrey reads my Postings and I don't really have to do a more amusing or wigged out one tomorrow. I may do none tomorrow. The sentence above is the last sentence in the Texas Gang novel. I had thought to write somebody tomorrow who has read TG, and had settled on Geoffrey, have not written him directly just lately.

Sorry to be fussing with you. Am having "strange moods" now. The trouble with telling you or many folks what I do tell them, is they do not know my passion, that, for example, I believe the USA is a police state, fascist. Will get worse, without action from the people suddenly. But you say I sound like one of the fanatical preachers etc. What if I am not lying.

Whatever I say, 911, Sandy Hook, Crop Circles, I am not lying. OK. I already HAVE BEEN trying to not talk directly to my siblings. If I do talk to others, who like as not agree with me fully, I should not have to use Blackbird Taboo-Speak.

And enough. Some of these folks much enjoy Mike Blackbird letters. And so on.

Jessica is here with Jake. I have yet to meet Jake. Kelly met me for dog walk, tried to get Jake to come too, Jake nearly did, Kelly says Jake changes his mind very much. Kelly has told me of boxing on a station I cannot get, and it is ten o'clock, at night. He gets it, was trying to get me to come over, "at least see an hour." Kept telling me I am welcome, though at this point his wife and daughter have been unfriendly. I said, well, Kelly, you know, I am a shy sort of person. Something, I said "shy sort of fellow."

We and dogs went down to the now thin Medina, and Kelly was pissed there were 2 stalled trucks, on the other side, but one had got to this strip more in the middle of the stream. I don't know why it was there. The other was plainly stuck. Heh, Kelly calls up the Fish & Wildlife authorities, whatever are they called, had also taken pictures of them, new tech, in as it is illegal to have vehicles in the stream, river. Kelly does not want any more trucks, etc. on the dinosaur tracks on our side. Yeh, Kelly wished for cloud burst, fix them then. He was though happy I am coming down through there every day with Choyota. And it is oddly warm, Bill still is in thongs and cutoffs. I might have my jungle hat on, they can think I am special forces. We know I scare others. If I say nothing. If I speak, riff raff sense I am cerebral. Less the threat, uh, perhaps. Oh, goddam, make myself laugh. Well, yes I know how to intimidate. But point here is, I said to Kelly, well, sure, I come through, but I feel like a bigfoot, am shy and just want to vanish in the foliage, float through. Yeah, these guys were out there yesterday and probably they saw my back.

Gone other way, a killer back certainly. Probably I have more childhood memory and impression than do others normally. I am shy. I got on when the other first graders discovered I was a good wrestler, easily best among the first graders in the little school. I hated school and did badly but realized around age 12 or so I was intelligent. Life went on and before adulthood I began to understand I was smarter in particular ways. I have sense of "relict hominid." People who know me know this of me. They are not using this terminology, relict hominid. My sense is folks are preferring to not think there - a form of taboo? What definitions do you want to use.

What was interesting before I thought to do one to Geoffrey is something had me in my cups google the last sentence in TG. Remarkably very much came up, many passages from books, some novels, some not.

First one was from this European author who if I am correct could not publish in his lifetime, name suddenly slips me, philosophical type fellow, cognizant of schizoid nation, renown for it.

I have not read him, but he is famous for this. He just never fell into my lap, I don't afford books. Some of this stuff might have his same problem, cannot find a trade publisher. They seem to be good writers, I could read them probably.

Oh, none had the Blackolive sentence, just that there was a hell of a reaction from one googling.

Hello, Geoffrey. You are very busy. Read TG in middle age sometime. Talk is fun.

Further,
Bill

Bix,

Oh, I do shit in the woods, daily. But on the dog walk to river. Carry paper towel, put that under rock or log when used. But to do first coffee crap, before walk, I would have to go to fence back of trailer to cross into woods. Guess I can do so when Bonnie is here. But you're right, why dig hole to shit in. Guess I was a bit foggy before finishing coffee.

Bix, maybe the woman you saw on tv is serious but I don't think she thinks Saddam did 911 or had weapons of mass destruction nor do I think she thinks Osama in his cave had it done. And if she does not think Osama did it, would she really think we just like to remove bad guys.

Could she not know we have a very long history of setting up mostly nasty people, to brutally rule, whom we can rule, in order we get stuff. Old Tom Jefferson said to young Monroe it is all ours down there! All ours! Manifest Destiny! Ah. Misprint. OK, Monroe Doctrine!

Saddam sounds like he was not so nice, but little as I search to know, Asad has sounded alright. He did not gas anyone. Why on Earth would he? Those he has been fighting with who have wrecked the infrastructure of Syria and murdered many people are groups run and supplied by the CIA, whatever they are called, different names for them, gassed a big camp of Asad's refugees.. These gangs are being killed at present, just lately, as Syria asked for Russia's help and has it, jet fighters. Now, Kadifi, he was truly alright, was doing very much for his people. What he was doing has not been in USA news.

Dug wells to turn desert green, gave cash to newlyweds etc. A well liked person. USA is very ugly.

Wesley Clark has talked how in his retirement he was shocked to find the USA plans were to take these several countries out. The Merchants of War and Big Oil are much the partnership. They profit no matter who wins a war. Meantime the USA does have large insane plans....

Well, like I said, re. Kadir Momand, an Afghani, the USA wants Afghanistan's abundance of Rare Earth Elements, REEs, of which the USA has little of - now needed for technology. Too, as he says, and also as another fellow I found today says, the CIA heroin business is huge. The other fellow, Asif Haroon Raja, is Pakistani, is an informed journalist and former military as is Kadir Momand. Kadir says he hates war, I expect Asif does. They are educated and handle English well. Both see the USA is losing grip. Putin knows it.

Interesting, Kessler has referred to himself as being a Liberal. Before looking at it all, he was for gun control. Now he is not. Outlaw guns outlaws have the guns etc. He points to the true statistics of other countries. The countries less violent are those where ordinary folks have plenty of guns. Obama is lying, says Jim.

I am sure Obama is lying.

Latest book Kessler is soon bringing out is NOBODY DIED AT SANDY HOOK. Gee, maybe he will send me a copy again. But, meantime, poor Obama is having a difficult time, or his handlers are: How to take guns from Americans? Wow, what a task.

Further,
Bill

QUOTE REMOVED BY ORDER OF DHS, UNITED STATES
DEPARTMENT OF HOMELAND SECURITY. [DHS US2FA]

What if I told you it was done with mirrors
What if I showed you it was all a lie

Hush, now don't you believe it
Cover your head and close your eyes
Now, take it or leave it
Go back to bed
Now don't you cry

What if you could've been there on
that day in Dallas
What if you could wrestle back the hands of time
Maybe somethin' could've been done in Memphis
We wouldn't be livin' in a dream that's died

Go on and tell yourself again there are no secrets
Go on and tell yourself that you don't want to know
It's best that you believe that you don't
hear the footsteps
That follow you around no matter where you go
Maybe you were thinkin' that it didn't matter
Maybe you believed nobody else would care

— Steve Earle, *Conspiracy Theory*

NINETEEN

"I do," said Evey.

The two stood holding hands with Jorge right behind them in his wheelchair with Rachel at his side, white flowers in her hair, gripping red flowers and wearing a new white dress featuring yellow flowers.

They were in the nursing home chapel with the minister and one of the nurses sitting at the organ.

The organ blared as Rachel tossed the flowers straight up and caught some of them, Evey and Blake kissed and Jorge dabbed a tear.

The next day they returned to the nursing home and everyone wore serious faces.

They gathered in Jorge's tiny room with the curtain drawn for privacy but his roommate hardly ever left, so.

"You shouldn't do this," said Jorge.

"I know, but," said Evey.

"Yes, we should," said Blake.

"We have to."

"You don't have to," said Rachel.

"We've got to feed Roswell, who's gonna feed Roswell?"

"We shouldn't have told her," Blake said to Evey.

"No, you should not," said Jorge, "never tell her you are leaving her, tell her something else, never that."

He wagged his finger.

"Where are you *going!*" Rachel wailed.

"We told you, hon'," said Evey, scrunching into a squat.

Blake closed the curtain all the way and peaked around. The man appeared to be sleeping, with eyes crunched so tight.

"We are leaving, dear," said Evey, now seated in a frail wood chair with Rachel on her lap. Blake and Jorge also sat, on metal folding chairs. Nurses hustled along in the hallway and now and again a resident in a wheelchair would pause outside the doorway searching for something, anything. The urine and medicine smell mixed with the eye-watering stench of the tiny beauty salon now in session down the hall.

"To protect you," said Evey.

"Ohhh, brooo-ther," said Jorge in perfect English.

"That is just what the soldiers say. It's just not true."

"But it is," said Blake, leaning out over his legs, knees with folded hands for emphasis.

"We are going …," he searched the inexplicable pattern in the tile for a guide.

"To stop all the bad things happening."

Rachel looked at Evey and Evey nodded.

Jorge saw his neighbor's bare feet and legs dangling from his bed, showing under the curtain, and he knew he needed to say something.

Jorge merely nodded at the curtain and Blake knew to get up and open it.

The man sat on the side of the bed in his flimsy pajamas falling off him everywhere, his WWII helmet on his head, staring at them with tears running down his face, just at the mention of the word soldier.

"You are staying here, with grandpa," said Evey, crying, her nose touching Rachel's nose, her hands framing Rachel's face.

Jorge wiped his face with the back of both hands.

Blake went to perch on the bed next to the man behind the curtain. He put his hand around the man's thin shoulders and pushed his helmet up straight just as it drooped.

They stayed like that, sniffling, not talking, while normal life carried on in the hallway, med carts rolling along, nurses calling for residents to come this way, you don't live that way, over here. A woman in white hair, just from the beauty salon, stopped in her wheelchair right in the doorway. She stared in at all the people with their heads down. The little TV on Jorge's neighbor's dresser was on silent, but it showed "The Price Is Right," a contestant guessing the wrong thing and having to sit back down. The woman saw it and stared, then looked back to all the sad folks, then grabbed the wall railing to pull herself along.

"So much sadness in the world," she mumbled, leaving a trail of hairspray smell.

It was all Evey could do to leave that room, to again pull out of a routine that while not easy was her routine, to actually leave Rachel, and her father, without anyone dragging her away, but to walk away herself.

Unimaginable. *Crazy.*

She thought.

She turned again in the hall and waved with both hands as Rachel stood in the hallway, next to Jorge's room.

Evey ran back.

She knelt down and hugged Rachel and wept.

She got up and ran the other way, past Blake, down the hall, out the door, where she fell to her knees.

Blake found her, sat with her, then helped her get up.

They saw into Jorge's room from the outside window as Rachel began to read a book to Jorge while a nurse walked in and helped the neighbor man get back into bed, set his helmet on the side table and close the inner curtain.

Blake and Evey took the bus to the city, to Eden Prairie, in the southwest suburbs.

The bus dropped them right at their hotel.

They let it go away and stood watching the busy city scene.

Evey sat on the bench.

"Let's go," said Blake, "right over there."

She just stayed, swinging her backpack between her knees.

"Evey.

"Evangelina."

"Why did you leave me," she said.

"What?"

"You know. You left me. To go do your thing."

She used knee-level air quotes.

He sat down.

Cars honked, more buses hummed past.

Finally she looked at him with tough eyes.

He looked back and then down and up again, this time at the sky. He took a deep breath.

"I don't know," he said.

Without looking she whacked him on his arm with the back of her hand.

They both rested back on the wooden bench with the advertisement for "The Prince Hope Show."

Evey shook her head and who knows what she was thinking.

After several minutes she got up.

Blake also stood, watching her to see what was next.

Evey yanked her bulky backpack up over one shoulder, stepped into the street and marched toward the hotel. At the door she held it for him to lead them inside.

They spent the night staring at the ceiling, listening to semi trucks and the ice machine, to kids with their parents, running down the hall, excited to be going swimming.

In the morning, they went down early to eat the free breakfast. They drank the coffee, studied the food then went upstairs to shower.

Blake and Evey double-checked their backpacks, each others clothes, and stared at a minute of local news, which was like watching a horror movie to their minds, at this time.

They knelt on both knees in the middle of the room floor. They held hands and bowed their heads.

"Hail Mary," Evey began, crossing herself.

The ice machine clunked. A jackhammer rattled. A car's horn beeped.

They double-squeezed each other's hand and pulled each other up.

The two went down the elevator, nodded to the front clerk and walked out to meet and greet the sun. They crossed the street at a break in the traffic and found a sidewalk to approach the one-story grey building marked just by a number.

Blake had been right, Evey thought. The backpacks were not out of line, lots of the others had them, and bike helmets, running shoes over shoulders.

They stepped into the flow, joined the tail-end of a group and headed for a door, wearing prominently their I.D. tags courtesy of Actually, who had returned to the cities from Hollywood to take his promised promotion at White Castle.

They nodded to someone at the door and entered the corporate world carrying not-colorful backpacks filled with hammers, screwdrivers, needle-nose pliers, toothbrush, toothpaste, extra underwear and socks.

Evey thought there would be bombs everywhere, tables they could overturn.

They padded along, in tennis shoes that did not really fit their church clothes, but they had told each other if we walk fast nobody will see our shoes.

What they found were offices and offices and hallways with more offices, a quiet efficiency. Everybody let them be, not glaring at them, except one guy and he looked weird anyway. People noticed them and went back to what they were doing, from the looks of it they were not out of place, which was disconcerting in a way.

Evey kept Blake's advice in her head, just act normal.

They stalked on, going fast, slowing down, eyes straight ahead, like secret agents in a movie and the accompanying music building.

Somebody was following them, the weird guy. Evey looked over her shoulder and saw him. She paused. Blake stopped, still facing forward, looking weird, feeling weird. Evey turned toward the guy and he walked past, forcing a grin, turned into a copier room.

Evey started again, looking straight ahead and there it was.

She marched right for it.

She froze at the steel double doorway.

The room, such a room.

It was the bombs.

Bombs on the floor, bombs on pallets, bombs in crates, bombs on conveyers, belts, whatever you call them.

Blake went right for one, sitting on the cement floor with its Rudolph-red nose cone.

Evey joined him there. They set down their packs as they had practiced in the hotel room, drew out hammers and started in smacking the bomb, not absolutely sure it would not explode. And then it didn't. So they hit it more, harder. Blake widened his stance and thumped it with hammers in both hands. Evey began to gouge at an edge with a screwdriver, thoroughly enjoying her work for the first time in her life.

Blake, breathing hard, said, "You'll ruin it that way."

"The bomb?"

"Nooo, not the bomb, the Phillips. I got that at Menards, not Walmart."

"Really? Blake? Seriously?"

Oh my god, she thought, someone still telling me what to do.

Evey got the top off, passed a tool to Blake as planned and they hurried with the needle-nose pliers cutting wires.

A crowd had gathered. While Evey kept working, now on her knees and getting a lot done, Blake took out a tiny bible and read from Isaiah.

Evey reached to her back pocket for her manifesto and then let it be.

The crowd pushed in closer and Evey stopped.

She stood beside Blake, pliers in her hand, sweat on her brow, breathing deep, through her mouth.

She felt calm, maybe from the good, hard work, relaxed. She looked into the eyes around her. They were scared, angry, confused. She wasn't. She recalled the day in school when she had forced her way into the big boys' circle on the playground to free the pigeon they had trapped under a box and let it loose. If they were not nine years old they would have killed her.

Now security pushed through the crowd, led by the weird guy, pointing.

Three now four men, now one woman too, worked to push the circle back while figuring out what exactly had gone on here.

Evey saw the guns on their hips. And she thought of the Prince Hope Show fake commercial for Gravitas Cologne, but she did not smile.

One of them talked into the machine on his shoulder, two worked with hands straight up in the air and waving to empty the entire warehouse work room, while the woman stepped in close to Evey with arms folded across her chest.

"So, you're crazy, right?" said the woman officer, smiling.

"Very much so," said Evey, grinning, nodding, "from the looks of it, huh?"

The woman had already turned away, mouthing the words, very ... much ... so.

More police arrived, these from the street, bigger, wearing hats.

Evey and Blake were handcuffed right there, in front of their tools and their dismantled bomb, photos taken by who knows who. Angry excited voices trying to sound corporate calm said lots of stuff on the intercom.

People walked past the door to the work room, looking in, apparently weren't supposed to stop and stare, they turned around, walked back, told others what they had seen, apparently.

While some kept guard on Blake and Evey other police conferred.

They came up with a plan, which must have been to walk "them" straight out of the building and into the waiting police cars with their lights flashing, with all the street traffic staring, turning around coming back to see what is that?

A traffic helicopter from one of the TV stations took off, headed for Eden Prairie, got lost in finding the right building, turned around, came back, got in as close as possible, filmed all the literally dozens of emergency vehicles, fire truck, ambulances, and police units of the different branches and municipalities.

With their blue and black uniform escort, Blake and then Evey, handcuffed behind their backs, were walked out of the big work room, where they had managed to leave, on the floor, next to their backpacks, by the bomb and the pliers and screwdrivers and hammers, a CRUSHER button, produced by Actually, like a candidate button, with the very orange "CRUSHER" on a white background, and a John Kennedy, red, white and blue campaign button that Actually had ordered online and that's it.

Still Evey was calm as they walked the worker gauntlet. She had practiced this in her mind so she had already done it, like an athlete running her race, she recognized every turn when it got there.

Some of the people said nasty things to them, but not loud, just right at them, making it personal, as they passed. Mostly it was quiet in the hallways, which were dark for some reason, as if they had decided that now they must preserve energy, watch the cost of everything.

Somebody clapped but only briefly. Mostly the thing was the looks on the faces, flashing in between the big shoulders of the big cops, like cars on the other side of the tracks as a train passes.

Evey felt the cold, hard steel on her wrists and it pinched the skin and dug in on her bone and she liked it.

Somebody bought a drink in the vending machine and it rolled and plunked hard.

She smelled rain, the earthy odor of coming or going or current rainfall and through it all a little breeze to stir the sweat beads on her forehead that told her maybe she was frightened out of her mind and her heart just did not know it yet.

The weird guy, with the fuzzed hair and white shirt, held the door dutifully for the cops and stared hard at Evey as she passed outside into the bright buzz.

Now came a flood of noise and chaos ... a door opened and the ocean let into the closet.

Lots of activity outside, photos, hollering, helicopter, car doors slamming, bustling, jostling, pulled this way no this way.

Rain.

Evey knew that right now the word was getting out.

It wasn't.

In Jorge's room, Rachel was reading or playing and just now realized, asked Jorge what time is it. Blake's parents poked heads into the hall for clock or nurse.

"I don't know," said Jorge.

"There's no clock in here, ask a nurse."

"I don't know, I'll check," said a passing someone in a blueish uniform.

Blake's father turned on the radio, and already, news of the event.

"Oh no!" said Rachel and pushed her thumb on 'send' on Evey's phone and the press release went out, almost everywhere, as Jorge's neighbor said "nine forty-two, where's my pills," from behind the curtain.

Evey and Blake were set into the backseat of a green and white Eden Prairie police car.

Each looked out their window at all the people gawking in, jostling, being moved back by police and ahead of them lights flashing. Evey strained to turn behind to see more cars, more lights more people and up on the freeway traffic stopped still. They looked at each other with wide eyes and then both straight ahead as their driver and the other got in, talked on the radio and pulled out slowly behind the other units, maroon and yellow state patrol, others ahead of that.

Blake mouthed "Wow!" to Evey and she mouthed "I know!"

They drove to the interstate entrance where foot patrol had opened a spot. Up high and clear they viewed the whole scene, people and cars and helicopters and flashing lights.

Their escorts didn't talk to each other or their prisoners, only to the radio microphone, and only once in awhile.

They came to an exit where again a space had been cleared.

Into a town, a suburb, a well-kept main street and a low brick structure, almost new marked City Building.

Already a crowd was forming here, running toward them. Their escorts hurried, got them inside a steel door, headed down a long narrow tiled hallway to a front counter not unlike the customer service counter at Walmart, Evey observed.

They were getting looks.

And Evey and Blake found each others eyes, to say, what the hell, they know, we're celebrities.

With police gathered all around, behind them, down the halls, behind the desk, Evey and Blake stood at the counter, emptying their pockets, giving their names, remembering so far not to mention Rachel.

One police woman, short, smart, and young and fit, behind the counter, attempted to take control, remain calm, like a good Walmart checker who everyone remembered and wanted to get, while all others around her were losing their minds and blaming it on her.

She smiled, first at Evey, then at Blake.

"Do you have any weapons?

"Do you feel like harming yourself?"

The phone rang and while the room was stuffed with cops, apparently it was also this one black woman's job to also answer the phone.

"No. We don't know anything about that. I can't tell you that. I can't tell you that either. No comment. Yes, have a good day." She chuckled quickly, shook her head and got back to work, quickly finding two envelopes for their belongings. Evey wondered how long it would be until she saw her half pack of gum.

The woman cop said something to each of them, inaudible to any of the surrounding officers, perhaps on purpose.

Then each of them felt a grip on an arm.

They leaned back over a shoulder, looked at each other and tried to smile as they were taken down different hallways.

Prince Hope shook his head and closed his eyes, *oh my god.*

Oh, My god.

He rubbed his fists into his eyes.

Oh, my God.

He practiced it a few more times and bowed his head, his nose almost touching his desk.

He heard his cue and did not move.

The red lights on the cameras blinked.

On thousands, no ... millions of screens, everywhere, viewers tried to figure out what they were looking at, the top of a straw hat?

Slowly the hat pulled back and revealed the full beard face of Prince Hope, red eyes.

"Oh My God."

"... this is against democracy and freedom, and it's just

bullshit behavior, pardon me. We must work together against forces coming at us from every direction and now this from right here in our heart, our soul, in Minnesota. It's the internet. We know that."

And then a commercial for Big Really Red Chevy Pickups. "Hoooh! Good God Y'all."

Everywhere people peeped out from behind curtains because they heard rhythmic running, like many troops marching outside their windows, and when they looked, they saw nothing. It comes from the sensory protectors now placed in the street lights, part of the privatized, out-sourced public works program called "Lets Be In Touch," where commercials can be broadcast in the neighborhoods when people choose not to watch TV or mow their lawns that they don't have to be out of reach. "Be in touch," says Prince Hope, as they go to break.

"I wonder what that was?" the people in the houses said to each other and then returned to eating toast.

QUOTE REMOVED BY ORDER OF DHS, UNITED STATES
DEPARTMENT OF HOMELAND SECURITY. [DHS US2FA]

1492.
As children we were taught to memorize this
year with pride and joy as the year people began
living full and imaginative lives on the continent
of North America. Actually, people had been living
full and imaginative lives on the continent of North
America for hundreds of years before that. 1492 was
simply the year sea pirates began
to rob, cheat, and kill them.
— Kurt Vonnegut, *Breakfast of Champions*

TWENTY

Washington and Korey stood by the shrine, shining the flashlight at all the various shit.

And yeah, it was cool at first, but now they went there just to do something, to get out of the Viet Cong kitchen and the living room.

That was the thing about being underground. It's dark. You couldn't have the electricity on all the time. You have to preserve. That's what Korey was always nagging Washington with anyway.

"The Woo," said Korey.

"Uh, Wu, uh, peed on the rug," said Washington.

"No. Woo."

"The Woo be with you."

"And also with you."

"I sense a disruption in the Woo."

They practiced their routine for when someone came to visit, like kids who had this one secret club where some day they will do cool shit and save people and it never happens with real people, and eventually you get older and move on to other shit, but for a while it's all right.

Mostly they sat and smoked and wondered what the fuck?

"No, seriously," said Washington.

"What was your original plan, man?"

They did manage to think about the treasure that Reuben and Hector found. They did have a map. Who gave Hector the map? Did he find it? Or what? Was the treasure homage to the Woo? In the Civil War? WTF?

Korey sat on a cane chair at the table in the kitchen in the cave shoving his coffee cup back and forth between hands like a hockey puck.

Washington lay with his arm over his face on the cot, by the doorway. The electric lights shimmied like they did a hundred times a day when a big truck goes over above.

They had even tried digging, expanding the underground under the whole United States for a place for people to go to escape the United States and have a whole 'nother country down there like somebody's vision a long time ago, but shit.

They were bored, with digging, with The Woo, with "havin' it goin' on like the Vietcong."

"Do you know anyone who raises chickens?" asked Korey.

"Answer as truthfully as you are able."

"What? … Fuck you. And what if I do? Is this a test?" said Washington.

"Is that going to be good or bad?"

Seconds passed.

"Yes, I do," said Washington.

"I see," said Korey. "I see.

"Do you know anyone who has ever seen a giraffe. Not in a zoo."

"Shut the fuck up," said Washington.

Something ran past the doorway, not making a sound and Korey saw it.

His mouth dropped open and he looked down at his coffee cup in his hands.

Seconds passed like more like two or three seconds.

"Do you believe in ghosts?" said Korey.

"No," said Washington.

"Do you believe in aliens?" said Korey.

"Fuck no," said Washington.

"Do you believe in Bigfoot?" said Korey.

"No way," said Washington.

"You're gonna have to change your ideas about at least one of those, I'm thinkin'," said Korey, "becauuse …"

"What … the fuck … was that?" said Washington, his arm still over his eyes.

"You saw it?" said Korey.

"Fuck yeah. It had a fucking face, man."

Washington sprang and sat in a chair at the table.

"It was a bear, man," said Korey.

"We got to get out of here," he said, reaching for his gun.

Washington grabbed a pistol and a shotgun from the gun rack and set them on the table.

"That was no bear," he said, now reaching for his AR-15.

"It was an alien, man," he said, grabbing his KABAR from his backpack.

"No way," said Korey, fitting on his brass knuckles and rolling his sleeves up over his biceps.

They decided what they had seen was a ghost, an old Indian, a Bigfoot, and an alien.

"The Woo," said Korey.

They found sidewalk chalk in the supply cave, used it to paint their faces, dressed up with feathers they found in the caverns, and began drawing on the walls, all the things they were feeling. They fasted, and burned something they found at the shrine that smelled like mint.

Korey and Washington sat on the cave floor by the white picket fence shrine.

They stayed up all night, hearing the scampering sounds and the "talking," and seeing the lights of the eyes down the hallways.

Look at this.

They discovered what looked like an old Indian pipe, more feathers, beads …

Washington and Korey could not tell day from night down in the underground. They remained on the cave floor by the white picket fence shrine for a long time.

They heard the chanting down the hallways and saw "spirits" come to them.

"I think it reveals a person's purpose in life," said Washington.

"Good people have faults, failures, foibles," said Korey with tears racing each other down his cheeks.

They drew a circle in the dirt and decided to stay in it.

The real damage is done by those millions who want to 'survive.' The honest men who just want to be left in peace. Those who don't want their little lives disturbed by anything bigger than themselves. Those with no sides and no causes. Those who won't take measure of their own strength, for fear of antagonizing their own weakness. Those who don't like to make waves—or enemies. Those for whom freedom, honour, truth, and principles are only literature. Those who live small, mate small, die small. It's the reductionist approach to life: if you keep it small, you'll keep it under control. If you don't make any noise, the bogeyman won't find you. But it's all an illusion, because they die too, those people who roll up their spirits into tiny little balls so as to be safe. Safe?! From what? Life is always on the edge of death; narrow streets lead to the same place as wide avenues, and a little candle burns itself out just like a flaming torch does. I choose my own way to burn.

— Sophie Scholl

TWENTY-ONE

After Actually left the Hollywood hill to go back to Minneapolis and the White Castle on Lake Street, Frida, Ike, Charlie, and Alice continued with the radio show over the computer while sitting behind tree branches and rocks and sandbags at the base of the HOLLYWOOD sign.

And now ...
We return ... to the continuing saga of ..."Behind Enemy Lines."

Tommy sits with his grandfather's ham radio on the old wooden work bench, a fire in the stove, flickering.

Tommy leans on two legs of the old chair to get close enough to see in the low light to fine-tune the old beast.

Fuzzy, humming reception.

Outside something walks past the garage, sucking mud, the rain patters on the ancient roof, a drip-drip pops the concrete somewhere in the dark.

Like a resistance fighter in France or Prague or the hills of South Dakota Tommy huddles in the garage.

The radio crackles, hums, buzzes, like it wants to talk.

Tommy wears the old leather headset, holds the rusty microphone to his mouth.

He pops a Cheeto into his mouth and drops one to Buddy at his feet.

What a time to be alive.

Bigfoot, conspiracies, UFOs, the vortex of human existence, the apex, the nadir.

He sucks on another Cheeto, time is growing short.

The fire pops, crackles along with the radio, the wind whips, the rain pounds.

"Tooommmy!!

The resistance fighter hears his mother and dashes for the door.

... *And now ... we join* ... in progress ... another episode of "The Americans."

The Americans is sponsored this week by "Operation Northwoods Deodorant," ... it hangs in the air long after you're gone.

... and also by "Go Your Own Way, Compasses For Republicans."

... as well as ... "I Think We're Alone Now Personal Computers, for Americans" ...

"The Americans" is also brought to us by Crisis Actors Of The Homeland, Operation Mockingbird, Operation Northwoods, COINTELPRO, and by Craft and Blackwater, bringing you Aurora, Tucson, Orlando, the Boston bombing, Sandy Hook, San Bernardino and so much more.

And now, "The Americans," ...

We re-join our reality show ... already in progress ...

... We see SpongeBlob Dr. StrangePants, the new "Secretary of Intelligence, Secrets and Prison Camps," working on his cabin assignments for the summer camp camp guards, er ... counselors, inmates, er ... campers. ... Are you ready for the summer? ...

... And in the Parallelogram Office we find Pres'dent Cosmo Nutt at his Big Desk working hard on his big clean yellow legal pad drawing pictures of dollar signs, boobs and tanks when in walks ...

... And, as we move closer toward "The Big Event" ...

In The Patsies Barracks located off the Rose Garden. ...

We find Rusty Kreikemeir from Hickory, Indiana on the roof getting ready to test his Phantom Menace costume and cape.

... The Director of the Big Event ... "Cecil B. de Propaganda," has just arrived at the helicopter pad on the lawn to meet with Cosmo Nutt and SpongeBlob Dr. StrangePants to discuss The Big Event.

Cecil B. has under his arm the 8x10 glossy photos and the three-ring binder and video telling all about "The Big Event & The Big Plan."

We then find ...

... the new GUARDIAN taking up residence in his new office in The White House basement next to the boiler room, dressed in his work clothes: tan pants, tan shirt, tan cap, nametag "Ralph" — like an actor playing a janitor in a sitcom in the 1960s.

His office door says "Maintenance Of Public Lies."

He takes the back elevator, the kitchen trolley, up to the Parallelogram Office, walks in Door No. 3 as The Child Left Behind sits under the desk, her dolls off to one side, writing something on a yellow legal pad.

The GUARDIAN steps up to the desk to talk to Pres'dent Cosmo Nutt.

The Child Left Behind can see the dust on the black shoes of The Guardian. She writes a note.

"So," says Cosmo Nutt.

"Whattaya got?"

The Guardian hands over a manila envelope.

"We need to maintain these public lies."

Cosmo Nutt opened the folder and drew out the papers.

He read the stamps on each of the documents:

"Yes," said Cosmo Nutt, "of course, of course, and how do we do that?

"What if we just told the truth, wouldn't it be simpler?" asks Nutt.

"Everything would fall apart," says The Guardian.

"Nobody would pay their taxes, nobody would go to work if they knew what is written in those documents."

"I see," said Pres'dent Cosmo Nutt, "well, please sit down and lets talk about each of these, one by one, in detail. I need to know just what's going on."

"Yes, of course, sir," says the Guardian as The Child Left Behind, sitting under the desk with her big yellow legal pad and lots of sharpened No. 2 pencils smiles wide and prepares to write.

I want to stay as close to the edge as I can without
going over. Out on the edge you see all
kinds of things you can't see
from the center.
— Kurt Vonnegut

God damn it, you're all gonna die.
God damn it, you're all gonna die.
Oh, Lord, God damn it, you're all gonna die.
— Elton John, *Texan Love Song*

It is such a splendid sunny day and I have to go.
— Sophie Scholl

TWENTY-TWO

About the only thing with color those days were the red in the Chevy truck commercials, the ubiquitous yellow ribbons, and the green and blue in the watery eyes of the children as they sat by the window with toys in their hands, watching it rain.

"They talk about revolution," said Prince Hope.

"Revolutionaries, manifestos.

"We must guard against the acquisition of unwarranted influence, that's what Eisenhower said. "And that's exactly what we have here. The types who go uninvited, unwanted into our businesses and begin to smash and destroy, seeking to gather others to the same sort of sordid enterprise. If that is your revolution for justice and peace, leave me out of it."

Hope then read a poem about lakes and little boats and sang a song about summer rain.

After the Chevy Big Red Truck commercial with the smiling, laughing troops in the back (Hoooh!), the big screens everywhere showed smiling Americans wearing their yellow ribbons that said "We Love The Rain."

Josephine Custer sat straight in the hardback window bus seat.

Her wrists were stuck together with duct-tape colored handcuffs.

The grey bus filled with prisoners headed for prisons around the country rolled along Colorado Highway 50 toward Pueblo.

Josie had already been to Alderson, West Virginia, Chicago MCC, Oklahoma City, and was now headed to Florence, Colorado.

She nodded once in a while as she listened to the woman next to her talk.

Paul Ciancia was recently sentenced to life in prison for the Los Angeles International Airport shooting of three years ago. Cia n Cia, hmm?

Isn't it interesting? All this.

We seem to be collecting quite a few people in prison for the on-going story of these hoax events.

They must carry on the story as if it were real.

Mousaaii, the so-called 20ᵗʰ hijacker, in Florence, Colorado supermax federal prison, Terry Nichols from the Oklahoma City U.S. government bombing, James Holmes, the so-called Aurora Theater shooter, the Tucson shooter, the Chatanooga shooter ...Dzhokhar Tsarnaev, the man who did not bomb the Boston Marathon... all of the ones who don't get killed or don't die the way they are supposed to.

You have to try these people, send them to prison and keep them there the rest of their lives. That is a lot of work.

How about Philando Castille – in Minneapolis. Do a Youtube search and start wondering if that was real.

And here's something:

Red Silver J: What You Need To Know About Paul Ciancia and the L.A. Shooting Hoax.

Yes, the alternative viewpoint is that they would not do this, not go to this trouble to carry it out, all the trials and such, but what other choice do they have. They are committed to the bit.

But we must also consider that they might, lie and carry through. Think of how long the lie of the JFK murder has gone on, tirelessly, endlessly.

Hmmm?

They have unlimited resources, money, control of the media, the spin, control over the patsies. You cannot imagine the pressure they can put to bear on you. Cannot imagine.

There are still many members of the Black Panther Party in prison, since the 1960s ... we only learned about COINTELPRO because of the Media, Pennsylvania burglary.

The FBI over the years has worked to undermine anything we ever put together that resembles a people's movement, The Social-

ists, The Wobblies ... peace movement, with Manson, the American Indian Movement, The Occupy Movement ...

Hmmm?

... Standing Rock ... these people, the FBI, CIA .. are committed ... if it's hard to imagine the U.S. being this way, just imagine the KGB, Russia, the American Russian novel all we need is more vodka thing ... you can imagine life in Russia being like that at least at one time, right?

Well, then it's definitely possible.

It's just that you don't know any Russian people. You did not go to Russian grade school. You didn't grow up on Russian sitcoms and Russian late night TV with Russian comedians.

You are here and you can't believe it is here.

It is. It just is.

It definitely is.

The woman sitting next to Josie looked at her closed eyes and closed her eyes too. Josie had already talked about meditating and the woman thought she would try it too. She tried, then fell asleep with her head on Josie's shoulder as Josie's head bounced on the window.

They rolled on down the little highway not hearing the rain on the windows and the roof.

The CRUSHER Trial, as named by Prince Hope, opened in downtown Minneapolis under low dark clouds, bowling alley thunder and Alfred Hitchcock lightning.

The cameras showed the rain in downtown Minneapolis, lit by the restaurant and bar signs and the flashing police car lights.

A black van pulls to the curb, immediately engulfed by the people, flashing lights reflecting the scene in the wet black metal.

Evey and Blake were hustled into the big grey stone building, out of the black van marked Hennepin County. Evey smiled at reporters as she was carried along, into the shined marbled hallways with Prince Hope's face on the many TVs on the walls, providing a live commentary.

Evey watched while Hope stared right at her as she passed, "here they come," as they were taken into the courtroom through the large wooden door on the first floor.

And in that courtroom a whole gigantic universe revealed itself, of the appearance of ideals and thought and reason and caring, like the basilica on Summit Avenue where the marathon finishes.

Each morning in America began like that, the same scene repeating.

With the help of Blake's parents, who also tried to be in the cities each day for the trial, after they moved Jorge and Rachel back to the farm. They put out pirate flags and let Roswell graze in the front yard with his Ojibwe alien blanket. They put up signs and flowers to show the graves of Reuben and Hector right where they had been shot and died, with Maria in the front flowers under The Virgin Mary and Pancho Villa.

QUOTE REMOVED BY ORDER OF DHS, UNITED STATES
DEPARTMENT OF HOMELAND SECURITY. [DHS US2FA]

I keep coming back to this song again and again. Steve Earle's history with drugs and addiction doesn't surprise me at all, his level of empathy is mind blowing and that must hurt him like hell, how many artists can do this? This is the pinnacle of singer songwriting talent, the story telling, the sensitivity, the empathy, the hidden nuances. What made him even think to do this? He managed to pull a story out of all the bias and fear and make it personal to his subject not just a load of white noise about preconceived notions.

— from the comments section

TWENTY-THREE

Billy in Iowa continued to write and to send what he wrote to everyone he knew.

Subject: the philosopher
Bring me to your heathen
and should I drink their wine
I will lend me yours
and take them thine

This is more how that poem goes. Yesterday I was having my wine. I see over the decades since THE TORTILLA HIKE I tend to be remembering the poem slightly different in wording.

It fit the note to you yesterday. If you were drinking or fretting something and missed it, see the word from yesterday again.

When I lived in the cabin, we had this small community of neighbors who would share labor if building somebody's house. I could dig or chop or something if I were given direction. One day I was standing in a place and a neighbor on a walk came by and looked at the several of us busy, and he said: What I want to know, is what is Bill's job.

Bill: I am the philosopher.

Neighbor: Oh, ok, well, thanks, I just wanted to know that.

Now, you, or Hatch know, were you at toil, and Bill staring at the mountains, and he said he is the philosopher, either of you would say you want to be the philosopher and Bill can work.

Mike Blackbird and I are sentimental about hunter/gathers. I will take pause sometimes as to did he firstly say this or that or had I read it first, or just knew it of course. We have, so what lies in school, had these fabulous technologies, before what is here this time, but probably still mostly we are genetically hunter/gathers.

There are no Big Chiefs. Nobody would take a Big Chief

seriously, had he no army behind him, and true hunter/gathers have no reasons for such. They must keep moving, ain't no payrolls. Anybody can be homosexual or a philosopher or anything else not dragging the travel. Bill would not have to do anything. Everybody would feed Bill.

They would do so were Bill no fighter at all. Why fuss about shit. Move on, physically we have to shift, follow the buffalo. Let me see here, Packy, we have War Chiefs, Peace Chiefs, Medicine People. Visionaries and so on. Mike did tell me, and it figured, hunter/gatherers are the most generous peoples on Earth.

Now Mike has not caught onto some numbers, the historic lies and relating. Not sure with Bonnie, Kelly, individuals hit sundry snags. Bonnie majored in Astro Physics at IU, later decided to be a movie star, then to write movie scripts. Wish you had rented the Aransas house, we are getting break ins, I have 2 manuscripts in a chest I have not other copies for, novels. And Kelly will fall back on we got to take care of business, pay our bills and so on, how about those Lakers, or what team I have per annually zero sense. Half a century and more I never know did the Colts win or who fucking won, at all, baseball, football, basketball. Amazing. I must be a philosopher.

In Aransas with Lyla alone was it a decade or more, in life of Medicine dog, who went to age of 16 or 17, a thing I was doing before and after getting online - to start Bonnie got me a computer a Xmas - was looking at History Channel stuff.

Much of this is accurate, like worldwide proof of previous technologies. University archeology is lies. Relict hominids. University anthropology is lies. Hell yes American History is lies. I have a sagittal ridge on my skull and could never stand on my head and I can beat hell out of any conservative university professor talking because my heart is pure, I can see. Help us all poor Jesus.

Alright. I must enter my third cup. Enough you can chew on, or not. Steve thinks to visit about now, come with Steve. Tell Richard, whether he could bring Jim.

In reality, I can say this. Take away from Jim his anti-psychotics. All, all, all, he will be a man who has reasonable bow-

el movements, a reasonable man. I know it. I am the seer. So fucking what.
FURTHER FUCKING OUT,
Bill

Mike,
In my memory the cops put the spotlight on you before we knew it was cops. Your self image was the cool fellow and before the cops asked you anything you said: Sometimes the moon is blue.

Heh, this is funny, your version and mine. Frankly, I can't remember these cops asked anybody anything. When this kid said the moon is blue they just figured fuckit, and left. As I thought about this yesterday, Hatch and Packy and I liked to bother strangers psychologically, pedestrians or motorists, and I think maybe one of us in a screech did leap from the window. I liked doing the rough stuff, hit the ground rolling in a howl. I bet Hatch or Packy might recall something of this one.

Teenagers seek identity. The fifties in the USA was manic-depressed anyway. I still am, but I stay weird, the anarchist. You during the sixties in Berkeley talked to me of your thinking in high school that a guy could be either physical, or intellectual. You said you had not figured it out, one might be both. Thus, you would be the smooth wit, with females. Another girl, from my class, one above yours again, was Etta Kay. Don't know if you remember, that later on she took a horrible car wreck, some brain damage, I don't know if she got back to normalcy. But she was of voluptuous build and another female with humor who would have been suited for the high school sixties. In lunch break she would be going your way, to our house, and Hatch tells of driving along and Mike is with Etta Kay being witty and she tosses back her head in laughter. Hatch mimics this. Kind of seems maybe Clair and Etta Kay were buddies...don't know....

I maybe could have been slightly less angry, could I have been a sixties kid. You and I both were a bit slow in maturing physically, unlike Kelly. Besides, asthma set me back. But my personality and atheism pissed off older guys. When I did have the boxing, thanks to B.E who coached the team, I was OK, before I weighed 150. Which scared the older jerks and one of them who might have weighed 150 I mauled age 18 in a satisfaction, very funny, I was bigger than him by 20 lbs. Anyway. I digress. Yeh, and I was reading Whitman and Kerouac and Henry Miller. Arrogance can help a kid.

Har har. Or grown man. A woman as well.

If I can stop digressing. Sure, circumstantial, environmental, much direction comes from our puberty. Cultures, of aborigines or city states or any sort, the kid takes a direction. We pass height of vigor too early. That is wrong, something is not right.

I see I no longer feel compelled to reproduce. Madrea has done well. She is about to spend a week in hospital with Zed, while they do some kind of EEG. I have to get money to her because she will not be able the week to do at the school cafeteria work or sub teaching.

We have to get to medical marijuana, meantime many old fart MDs are reluctant to give a script for it. I always have zero respect. But we will get there. Zed is a marvelous vitality. Her 3 kids are. I do like Emily, from Eli's first woman, who did some jail and so on. Emily is with that side right now, but wishes to not see Eli. Not to digress, I had been thinking I should beat up Eli's sad father for bringing him up stupid, both of them want to kill dogs. And on, and on. Ah, Eddie, the father, in his fifties, he is just another lost bastard, but maybe learns a little.

Sorry, I am slave to my story.

Anyhoo, I remember, Mike Blackbird was a funny kid. Did well in circumstance. This day is a new one.

Love,
Bill

Mike,

OK. I can repeat, for you and awful Packy who lost faith. I have been at this years.

We have a cosmos. We are not mechanistic. Mechanistic tells us zero. Makes no sense, is purely impossible. Look at this. Try sometime to make mechanistic make any sense.

I know, if I talk about official archaeology we have is impossible, under present terms, all of you have never thought will not think.

Relict hominids and UFOs get proven over and over and over. Some of you have never heard mathematical logic so should I continue to argue math, in a cosmology? This gets to be undignified. You either do it by yourself, or die. Try it next incarnation. I got no patience. I been at this years. What the hell do any of you imagine I have been doing but jackoffing. I do not jackoff. Out grew that shit. Patience is gone, man. You will not awaken.

Length, height, weight, what does it weigh, what can it sell for. You think that is real.

This author I am happy with is trying to tell his wife what he has been reading about the first 3 days of the Big Bang. In this bush a Bigfoot is laughing, "like a gorilla." I go with that one. You like science fiction, too bad. This one is real. Length, weight, height, and what does it weigh and what can you get for it is absurd, Mike Blackbird.

All you people want to think I spend years in my study jacking off. I be disgusted.

Either Way You Like It,

Bill

PS DID YOU NEVER EVEN HEAR THE GUYS LOOKING THROUGH SHUTTLE WENT CONFOUNDED. Oh well. Spectacular.

Yo, Bill:

Thanks, for the recapitulation of things past. I didn't remember that you were the guy, going through Richard and his father, that got Ray Stanford to come over and give the talk in Prairie, at the Lion's club.

Yes, I remember us going with them and the Prairie Ridge guys to a camp out at night. We had a fire and tried to call the Flying Saucers in. I recall feeling a bit pissed off, when they didn't come. Well, actually, I wasn't real sure that they existed, in the first place.

But, nonetheless, I felt that, if they did exist, then, they were ignoring us. Screw them, either way, I figured. Existent or, non-existent.

In retrospect, looking back on that night, it seems odd to me that, even though I wasn't sure they were real, I got pissed off when they didn't come.

I guess, I was hoping they were real. It would have been neat to see them.

You have probably heard that, in recent years, the astronomy data on how life might get started on other planets has become quite impressive. Basically, it's all chemistry--astronomers, now days, are pretty sure you have the right compounds floating around in outer space. Most of the serious astronomers now believe that life is fairly common across the Milky Way galaxy. The big question is, how often do you get intelligent life?

Lots of unknowns here; in particular, we know very little about how long it takes life to get complex, to evolve into real intelligence.

I figure, mammals are pretty smart. So, using that as a standard, it took earth a bit more than 4 billion years to evolve intelligent life.

Best guess, our universe is about 13.7 billion years old. The Milky Way galaxy is at least 10 billion years old. If 4 billion years is the normal length of time to evolve pretty good intelligence, then, most likely, this has already happened dozens of times, here in the Milky Way.

Of course, the Milky Way is pretty big---Probably, at least a 125,000 light years in diameter. That is, light photons take about 125,000 years to go across the Milky Way.

There is some math and physics suggesting that nothing will ever go faster than the speed of light. So, it would take even the fastest space ships years and years to travel anywhere in the Milky Way. If intelligent life is a rare phenomenon, and, given the size of the Milky Way, then, I think we'd have to have a lot of luck, to get close neighbors. Odds are the nearest intelligent entities would be at least a thousand light years away. That's a very long ways to go, just to say hello.

Some astronomers are afraid of the Others in the Milky Way. They think that, probably, our technology is primitive, on a galactic scale. So, it is much better to hide out here in the boondocks pretty far from everybody. We need some time---a couple thousand years, to spread out in the local star region. Learn a lot more. Get strong, so that we meet the "Others" on a more equal footing.

Well. The astronomers study hard. They have really good telescopes now days. And, we know more physics and, astro-chemistry. But, all of them will tell you--we are vastly ignorant about stars and, the Milky Way. No one, for example, really understands things like the super massive Black Hole that sits in the middle of the Milky Way galaxy. And, of course, no one understands the Dark Matter-Dark Energy problem.

We have a long ways to go. But, reading astronomy is fun. New data is coming out every year. Like I say, those guys are working hard. I got a few more years, to enjoy reading this stuff. Then, death comes.

Well, too bad. Got no choice, though. I'll just enjoy whatever years I got.

take care of yourself
Mike

There was no point in seeking to convert the intellectuals.
For intellectuals would never be converted and
would anyway always yield to the **er, and this will
always be "the man in the street." Arguments must
therefore be crude, clear, and forcible, and appeal to
emotions and instincts, not the intellect. Truth was
unimportant
and entirely subordinate to tactics and psychology.
— Joseph Goebbels

TWENTY-FOUR

Meanwhile, America continued to hear "The Americans" through a little static from the base of the HOLLYWOOD sign:

Meanwhile ... Downstairs ... Pres'dent Cosmo joined Mrs. Nutt at The Big Formal Camo Ball at the welcoming line.

Mrs. Nutt told everyone how she loved what they had worn, the various formal camo attire.

The child left behind by the previous administration or the administration before that looked as always out from behind a curtain.

Slappy The House Alien had decorated his antennae in camo.

He filtered among the guests with a tray of out of this world little delicacies.

Tom The All-American Sniper, in full camo including face paint and a helmet covered in leaves and grass, shook Mrs. Nutt's hand and complimented her on her see-through camo gown and camo tiara.

The Minister of Defense was allowed out of his kennel for the ball. He played with Vice-President Toad who tossed a ball and The Minister of Defense chased it.

Buzz The Space Dog arrived wearing a camo space suit.

Ricardo The Space Cat wore nothing at all.

Skippy The Construction Worker observed all of this as he looked in through the window, peeing in the Rose Garden, smoking a cigarette, on his way to the bar after he put everything away.

Join us next week, for another episode of The Americans where we find ... Ricardo The Space Cat say to Buzz The Space Dog ... "did you ever really talk to Neil Armstrong? What was he like?"

... And in the Parallelogram Office we find Pres'dent Cosmo Nutt at his Big Desk doodling on a legal pad, trying to figure out the whole Fukushima Thing, losing interest and instead drawing spaceships that are *dot-dot-dot* firing down at the White House, while under that desk is The Child Left Behind playing with her dolls and Slappy The House Alien downstairs trying to phone home from the newly installed payphones in the staff locker room.

...And, as we move closer toward "The Big Event" ...

In The Patsies Barracks located off the Rose Garden. ...

We find Rusty Kreikemeir from Hickory, Indiana.

He is just now getting the briefing on his new character "The Phantom Menace," on a need to know basis.

He isn't really told anything, he is just getting fitted for the costume, because he doesn't need to know.

Join us next week, for another episode of The Americans where we find Wayne Rambo, The New Secretary of "The Department of The Undermining of Social Movements and Groups," arranging on the wall, the stuffed heads of AIM [say AIM, not A-I-M], the Black Panthers, The Peace Movement, The Wobblies and The Democratic Party .

QUOTE REMOVED BY ORDER OF DHS, UNITED STATES
DEPARTMENT OF HOMELAND SECURITY. [DHS US2FA]

... all reduced by the towering structures around them to the size of insects, but scuttling, hurrying, intent in the milky morning sun upon some plan or scheme or hope they are hugging to themselves, their reason for living another day, each impaled live upon the pin of consciousness, fixed upon self-advancement and self-preservation. That and only that.
— John Updike, *The Terrorist*

TWENTY-FIVE

After many days in the circle, sweating, without water, food, seeing visions upon visions, hearing everything in the universe and travelling through outer space and time, Korey and Washington crawled on their stomachs by elbow and knee, plowing rows with their chins, back to the Vietcong Kitchen Nook as the hand-stitched sign said on the wall.

Korey hurled open the lid of the cooler, stuck his head inside and stuck it down lower until he hit his nose on the bottom.

"It's fuckin' empty," he managed a hoarse whisper.

"Fuckin' goddamn vision bastards," whispered Washington.

The radio was still on low in the corner, and at least one of them thought, without saying, oh, maybe that's what I was hearing.

Washington crawled over to turn it up when he heard "Blake and Evangelina."

"Fuckers," said Korey, sitting at the table with empty cans in both hands, peach juice running down his chin and sweat in his eyes.

"I'm fuckin' doin' it," he said.

They had long talked over the previous days about how Korey was going to return to Minneapolis and dressed as Geronimo scale the Foshay Tower like King Kong and fight the fucking bastards.

Korey told Washington that he had scaled the wall inside Gander Mountain with his scout troop and they even had to stay overnight in the store hanging on the plastic wall and had to listen to store sounds in the dark all night, so he was pretty sure he could do this.

And he had pinions and a bag to sleep in, all the needed shit.

It had seemed like the thing to do and totally doable a

few days ago at three-twenty-seven a.m. though they had no clock, but that's what it seemed like.

And after a few cans of pears and peaches it still seemed like a good idea to Korey.

"Nope," said Washington.

"That's crazy."

He set out peach cans and pear cans in various positions on the wooden Vietcong table.

"See. Over here. Is reasonable thought and action. It's what people do. See.

"And ... over here, here is crazy. It's what some people do. But they are crazy.

"What you are talking about is well within the boundaries," he drew a Venn diagram in the dust, "the confines and corridors, of pure grade, one hunnerd percent, crazyasfuck."

"That might be," said Korey.

And they made plans to find shit for Korey to wear to portray Geronimo, Gerry, Napoleon Ulysses Custer while scaling the Foshay Tower. They looked for other shit that might help him to actually climb a straight up building and they got whatever they had found out to the entrance to the underground caves of Reuben and Hector and then sat down to wonder how they were going to get to Minneapolis.

***

By this time Josephine Custer had become a full-fledged inmate of the United States Federal SuperMax Penitentiary in Florence, Colorado in the foothills of the Rocky Mountains. She had her private cell, stainless steel sink and toilet, and a number, and uniform and a door with a narrow vertical window through which she could relax on her bed and view the grey concrete block wall on the other side of the hall for the rest of her life.

She arranged her long black hair into pigtails and sat there, tall and straight on the edge of that bed, and closed her eyes. She automatically brought her hands together with her wrists touching and breathed deep.

She smiled and breathed deep and did not open her eyes, but continued to grin because somewhere someone on the cellblock had fought long and hard to get sage to burn and it was drifting her way and finding her, under the heavy metal door.

Foshay Tower was the lifelong dream and name-sake of Wilbur Foshay, an art student turned businessman who amassed his fortune by building up three utility company empires (operating as the W. B. Foshay Company). At the time the tower was being built, he had sold his previous two empires in turn and was building up his third (which was eventually to stretch from Alaska to Nicaragua). He planned to locate his business and residence on the twenty-seventh and twenty-eighth floors where a three-bedroom, three-bath suite was built, with a fireplace and library, Italian Siena marble walls and glass-paneled ceilings.[2][3]

The exterior is faced with Indiana limestone, while the interior features African Mahogany, Italian marble, terrazzo, gold-plated doorknobs, a silver and gold plated ceiling, ornamental bronze, hand wrought iron and three commissioned busts of George Washington.

It cost US$3.75 million to build. From the Marquette Avenue side of the structure, the name, "Foshay," is visible in concrete four times on the exterior of the building (once on the top and three times on the street level)

Indiana limestone has also been used in many other famous structures in the United States, such as the Empire State Building, the Pentagon, Yankee Stadium, and the Washington National Cathedral. In addition, 35 of the 50 state capitol buildings are made of Indiana limestone.[3]

Foshay invited 25,000 guests to the dedication ceremony and provided all-expenses paid trips to many who included cabinet members, senators and congressmen. Half-nude dancers entertained. Each guest received a gold pocketwatch.

The military gave 19-gun salutes. John Philip Sousa conducted music, including the "Foshay Tower–Washington Memorial March," a march he wrote for the occasion. Foshay presented Sousa with a check for US$20,000.[2]

The march was only played once during Foshay's lifetime. Six weeks after the building's opening on November 2, 1929, Foshay's corporate empire was thrown into receivership at the onset of the Great Depression. Ignominiously, Foshay's check to Sousa bounced, and in retaliation, Sousa prohibited the playing of the march so long as Foshay's debt to him remained outstanding. Foshay never lived in his new home, which also went into receivership. It wasn't until 1988 when a group of Minnesota investors repaid Foshay's debt to Sousa's estate that the march was permitted to be played in public again.

— Wikipedia

TWENTY-SIX

Each morning began the same for Blake and Evey as they were awakened early by a guard, taken out to a table in the pod and given a tray of coffee and cold cereal, then hurry to get dressed and wait to be called to the sally port to be taken by guards together down the elevator to a holding pen until the U.S. Marshals arrived to transport them to court.

Blake and Evey were able to talk each morning as they were taken to court in the black van.

Each of them had a mental list of things to discuss and they started right in, not worrying about whether their guards inside the van would let them talk. The guards in front didn't pay any attention to them, rather involved in their own discussions about their personal hopes and worries for the day.

"I think the attorneys should bring this up ..."

"Did you see so and so in the courtroom yesterday? Wow. ..."

"I should feel nervous, so many people, but I don't feel nervous at all. How 'bout you?" ...

"How is your food? Are you alone? ..."

"I'm not bored at all. I feel so busy ... and hopeful. This is working."

"I guess I don't get that. ... I don't see that. ..."

The guards had taken to putting umbrellas over them as they were taken out of the van and into the courtroom, serving a double purpose of keeping the two famous defendants out of the cameras.

They spent most of their day in court, getting a sack lunch together in a place off the courtroom, then brought back for the afternoon. They waved to the regulars, the ones who smiled.

They listened to the attorneys, and the witnesses who had watched them destroy the bomb. The "weird guy" gave a particularly detailed testimony and opinion, which was objected to by the defense attorneys but allowed in any case by the judge.

The Pres'dent had asked to meet with Prince Hope in the playground off the Rose Garden.

"I don't know," said Hope as he sat down to swing.

"Know about what!" yelled the Pres'dent who was already high in the air.

"Oh, you know, the usual, live or die, when's it gonna stop raining, what's wrong with the Twins bullpen."

"What?" yelled the Pres'dent, leaning back and kicking high.

Prince Hope twirled his swing tight and let it go, getting a blur of The White House, the helicopter sitting on the ground and a bunch of really red roses.

He stomped one foot down as he became dizzy.

The Pres'dent kept swinging so Hope walked into The White House to talk to the guards and see if he could get some coffee. …

"Right here," said Korey, setting down all his shit on the sidewalk.

How did they get there? From The Underground to downtown Minneapolis? Oh, that's a whole 'nother story right there. And we haven't got time … we do?

Billy and The Callwell Boys brought them, or they stopped by and asked if they could ride Roswell, or Prince Hope just happened to send them a limo, which makes no sense, but then again it does. Or they just Wooed there. Or they had this incredible Hobbit adventure with, well, lots of shit.

No mostly shit like that does not happen in real life. If you look around hoping for something really cool to just happen to you it won't.

But if you stick out your thumb you might get a ride. Shit like that does happen even though when it does it might seem like a miracle to you at the time.

Or maybe that doesn't happen at all and not every little detail is known about your life, how you got from here to there is not known to everyone and everybody.

And sometimes it just doesn't matter how you got here.

What matters is that you are here.

Washington leaned back to look up.

"Nice day," said Korey, working in a big hurry to get ready.

"Geezuz *fuck*," Washington said.

"It'll be fine," said Korey. "I YouTubed it."

"You YouTubed it," said Washington.

"Yeah-yeah, let's go, let's go!"

"Not me," said Washington.

"Yeah, I know, I know," said Korey. "You stay down here and hold the rope."

He handed Washington a rope.

"What do I do with this?"

He looked straight up and then at the rope.

"Yeah," said Korey.

"Okay, leave the rope here, we might need it."

"Okay," said Washington.

A crowd began to gather.

"I got to get up so they can't take me down."

"You just wrote the perfect country and western song."

"I did?"

"No. Better get going.

"And I'll be right here so they can at least arrest somebody."

"Right. Yeah, I guess. Here, I got to get going. Here, here.

"There, read that," said Korey, pointing to a plaque on the side of the building.

"I don't really ...", said Washington, wandering over toward the plaque, holding the rope, kind of watching Korey with his "climbing moccasins," and feathers and hair in a braid and war paint on his face and arms and a bicycle helmet with the feather poking out the top, orange CRUSHER T-shirt and wrestling singlet.

"S'posed to resemble Washington monument, that's you."

"That's me. Yep, okay, that's me. Go, go. Shit, here they come."

"You got to block for me."

"Block for you?

"You look like Spiderman!" said Washington after reading a couple of paragraphs on the plaque.

"I do? It's supposed to ..."

"No. No, not really.

"You look just like who you are."

"I do?"

"Yeah. Yer fine. It's okay. Don't think about it, just go. Go. You'll do great."

He hurried over to give Korey a boost up, folded his hands together for Korey to take his first step. He searched the crevices and ledges, finding another, and another.

Washington watched him go up, a little quicker than he thought he would. Washington held the rope.

Inside, in the Foshey Tower Lounge, some of the early drinkers turned on their stools with their elbows on the bar to watch "the funkadelic window washer" commence his ascent.

Jorge and Rachel headed off with Roswell past the rundown shed toward the back pasture.

Rachel sat high on Roswell as Jorge walked along slowly behind, his head down, looking for things to trip over.

They kept the radio cranked in the kitchen window. They walked all around the pasture and had a lunch out by a big tree and returned in time to catch the afternoon updates about the trial on the radio, the things they had not heard even with the radio on full-blast.

Korey's face scraped the stone face of the tower. He was already injured. It burned and sweat migrated into the wound, because of course it does. Limestone in an open sore. That can't be good. He felt the crowd growing below, the voices, some honking. He couldn't step back and see where he was, where his feet were, his hands. He had to go on feel and by straining his neck and by not thinking about falling and dying or maybe dying on the way down from fright and then hitting the sidewalk.

A spider scurried up the wall right in front of his nose, stopped, kept going.

"Hey, I'm climbing here!" Korey said to the spider in mind speak and watched it climb up, up, so easily.

It would be harder than the water, hitting the pavement,

even though some said that hitting water from high up feels like hitting cement. Korey stopped climbing, but did not stop gripping the stone. He was going to cut his fingers and legs all to shit, that much was for certain, and his face, his nose mostly, oh, and his cheeks, yep, his chin. He didn't know that before. But now he knew. He knew a lot more about climbing than he did ten minutes ago, that's for sure.

He thought about hitting his head on the sidewalk while he clung to the side of the building. Woah. Would it hurt or not? Prolly not, it would happen so-fucking-fast, but probly, fuck, yer hitting your fucking head on cement. *God* that's gotta hurt. Like a watermelon, just like that. So much blood. Oh, man. There was no getting around that.

And he was gonna get tired. You could not rest, not for a moment. You had to strain every-fucking-thing to stay focused and right up against and attached to this building.

And each step, each move was going to take courage, to go from what was kind of working to what he didn't know if it was gonna work at all, with his right foot, oops, that put some strain in his left hamstring, okay, where can that foot go, okay, yeah, that's a little better.

Now for my right hand, nope that won't work, no leverage, there, bring my left hand up, but where? Where goddamnit I'm gonna die! I'm dying here! Okay, okay, that's good. I like this. This is a good spot.

Korey strained to look up.

He was right fucking below a ledge.

There are ledges! Who knew? He would be able to rest and not die on ledges.

He was so close to the ledge he could not see it. He pushed up and bumped it with his head. This was where he would die for sure, pushing back enough to get up and around the ledges. And then falling.

He would need to remember to put out his arms and legs to make his fall seem more like those sky divers who are smiling and waving at the camera. He knew he would forget. He never remembers that shit.

He thought about being a good person. Maybe that was

why he was up here on the side of this building trying to be a good person, to do something good. To sacrifice himself. He had foibles, failures, faults. And those memories were more than willing to come charging on stage if the light got shined in their direction, to do their little dance, hey, look at me.

If his skull erupted down below like a volcano, getting *yechh* and brains and goop, poop on the people, brain poop, would all that be gone? Expunged? He'd like to think so, but Korey was not that lucky. It would probly be just one more thing to think about until time ends. But time never ends. Heaven never ends. He didn't want to think about that right now. He thought about, woah, he could not think about that shit up here. That shit ain't gonna work. He thought about baseball ... better.

Korey stopped, took a deep breath. Oh, and he was gonna itch all over. Oh man, he never thought about that. When he sweats he itches. And when he thinks about itching he itches. If you think about itching, scratch that itch and wait like one second, there is another spot that needs itching. It never fails. He was gonna itch like crazy.

Korey reached one arm up and felt the ledge. Yep it was flat up there. It was like heaven, probably, to be up there on the ledge, safe, resting, able to look around, itch your whole body, take a drink of ... *oh shit, goddamnit!* Fuck it. He was gonna die anyway. Your blood must go a long ways when it explodes on the sidewalk like a balloon, a watermelon balloon. God.

Okay, he reached the same arm up there again and made sure both feet were firm wherever the fuck they were, he had no idea. He reached the other arm up, one foot slipped and Korey almost blew up his head. He grunted and blew air like a weightlifter and his eyes got big and both feet were hanging loose and now kicking and he threw and pulled himself up on the ledge which was not that big and he lay there, staring out into space.

"Wash!" Korey yelled.

"Can ... you ... see me!"

"Dude," said Washington.

"You're like ten feet."

Korey looked down, over the ledge. He wanted to say twelve. Twelve-thirteen feet, prolly.

"I'm like right here," said Washington.

"Need anything?"

"No," said Korey.

"I'm good."

Washington passed out the leaflets, dropped some on the ground, set some on the tables in the two cafes right there, under the salt, on the counter, dropped some on the floor.

So far it wasn't raining. He thought about that when he dropped the leaflets on the sidewalk.

When he went back to stand underneath Korey the leaflets were either picked up or blown away. There was a little wind. That couldn't be good on a climb that's supposed to be thirty-two stories straight fucking up, unless he fell from lower down that is, and his fucking head detonated, went kablooey, and probably his arms and legs came unattached, who knows what happens with that kind of shit?

Washington saw some people reading the leaflets.

Korey began to depart from the first ledge.

Washington heard some low, like, mumble-chanting, like someone making a joke to a friend.

"CRU-SHER ... CRU-SHER."

What the *fuck*? he thought.

And then it stopped.

Like a sloth Korey moved straight fucking up. He couldn't get over how fucking straight fucking up this was. Shit. A sloth stickworm. And his underwear was all up in and not straight ... and he ... *God*-damn-it. Sweat ran in his eyes and it burned. He licked his lip and tasted salty sweat. It tasted like shit.

His shirt was all up from sweat and shit on his stomach and he rubbed his belly on the stone, and it didn't really bug him because he had just bumped the top of his head against some fucking jagged something that he would punch if he was on the street because, goddamn it! that hurt! Fucker.

Korey slithered and struggled to The 2nd Floor. There were windows. He knew there were windows. He had not thought about windows. He balanced on the ledge, his arms full-stretched-out to find edges … to cling to … for dear life.

His chest rose and fell as he breathed hard, sucked air. He had convinced himself it was harder to breathe at this altitude. He jumped and his heart went to his knees as a shiver ran through him and his life flashed through his brain and he dug his hands in even more at the same time when he saw faces on the other side of the glass, right there, inches from him, blank faces staring at him.

Korey thought for a split-moment he had come across a mannequin storage something, but these were real faces.

He felt self-conscious now. The faces just stared. They were people in business suits holding their coffee and watching him, kind of interested in him, kind of just looking out the window to not have to be at the whatever was going on in there with the long tables set up and the projector and donuts.

At The 5th Floor: Bird shit, all the fuck over the wall and on his arm most likely from that sea gull right up there, the white and grey one with the darting eyes, Korey thought. He wiped his sweaty arm and rubbed bird shit all over his CRUSHER tattoo. The sea gulls hovered all around him, taunting him like Satan with their cries, come off that wall, you can fly, just like us, if you try. *Try.* Just try, to fly. We don't know why. You cannot fly. That came into Korey's head and now he couldn't get it out, like the Barney song. And now, sprinkles, big drops that kind of washed off the bird crap. A helicopter, more concerned probly with traffic and weather than with Korey.

Korey would not look down but he felt the gathering of emergency vehicles below, like ground vultures, including an ambulance, and a bigger crowd now in the Foshay Tower bar pushed against the window looking right up and mostly laughing.

Jorge went for a walk by himself down the gravel road, just as Korey began to gain a little confidence, thinking he had this figured out and it was very doable. Jorge walked slowly, each move a possible fall. He searched for big rocks to fall on. He took one step then another, his hands finding things to do in the air. Korey's hands began to find holds without even really trying, boom-boom-boom.

Rachel was still sleeping and Jorge had always been able to make it to the one mile road and back again before she woke up.

He came to the house with the northern pike mailbox and saw the two sisters, hair dyed red and so rickety they could barely stand, sifting through their own trash, the regular and the recycling, like two finicky bears. He opened his mouth to say a word and then it just did not come out.

In Hollywood, at the base of the HOLLYWOOD sign Alice, Charlie, Frida, and Ike got ready to do their nightly show, "Live From Hollywood."

In the courtroom Evey again thought of Rachel and she lowered her head. Blake saw her and put his arm over her shoulder.

As Korey almost reached The 10th Floor, Washington dug in their backpacks for food, thinking that maybe there would be apple raspberry kiwi granola bars on the bottom. He pulled out a walkie-talkie.

"Is this on?" he said.

"Korey.

"Come in Korey. Earth to Korey. Space to Korey. … Earth to Maniac. Earth to Woo-nuts, come in Fucknuts. Commander Korey this is Earth Camp … this is Ground Control to Commander Korey.

"Is this on?

"Is this on?" he heard himself at the bottom of the other backpack and did not like how his voice sounded.

He put the walkie-talkies to both ears and spoke.

"Shit," he said.

Korey sat on The 10th Floor Ledge. Not every floor had a ledge, but when he came to one, he could sit and rest. Somehow he resisted looking down.

He looked up and he looked straight out and he lay down, but that weirded him out bad, it just did and he could not lie down for long, though he always tried it when he could, to see if it was still the same. Like, wow, too much to think about, too much of your head and the building and clouds doing spinny stuff and too close to falling.

So sit the fuck up, stare straight ahead or lean your head back against the building and close your eyes for a short while and that's about all you can do.

"Hey.

"How's it goin'."

Korey leaped.

He jumped forward and back and sideways and up and down and out.

"What!"

His eyes shouted.

Washington crawled on the ledge toward him on his hands and knees.

He sat down next to Korey, who could not speak.

"Fire escape," said Washington.

On the other side, connects right here.

"Here."

He handed over one of the walkie-talkies.

"Oh, yeah," said Korey.

"I brought those.

"Come in, Wash."

They both heard it in the other walkie.

That's how I sound? said Korey with his eyes without saying anything.

"Ever look down?" said Wash.

Korey shook his head and said yep.

"Got the rope," said Washington.

"Yeah, keep that, we might need it."

"Yep. Thinkin' 'bout gettin' a tattoo," said Washington.

"Full-face Loon. A loon, green, black, white, red eye."

"Yeah? They don't have green."

"Yeah. Yes they do."

"Pretty sure not."

"Epic."

"Yeah.

"Well," said Korey.

"Yeah, I should ..." said Washington, "you be careful, bro."

He held out his fist for knuckles and Korey double-tapped.

"That's cool," said Washington. "I've never really seen anybody do it that way."

"Yeah, somethin' I'm tryin' to get goin'," said Korey.

"You got a lotta shit goin' on," said Washington, "lotsa irons in the fire," he said as he crawled on his hands and knees the other way and Korey said don't tell anybody about the fire escape, bro.

Prince Hope returned to his office, bored, dejected, looked out the window, sat down, put his feet up, pulled up a droopy yellow sock and saw Korey.

That's Korey, he said out loud, bringing his feet down.

Prince Hope clomped out of his office in his blaze orange flip-flops to the elevator, rode it with the janitor who did not seem to know who he was, and out the revolving glass door into the sunlight so bright he had to search for his sunglasses on the top of his straw hat. He itched his beard and wiped sweat from his forehead as he walked right across the street, dodging traffic a bit, making them dodge him a little. He wore white shorts and Hawaiian-type shirt, yellow, green, pink-ish, whatever the fuck they look like. He slapped his way into the crowd looking up. Someone handed him a leaflet and he read it, and it wasn't bad, parts of it.

As Hope followed his path to return to his office Washington finished his descent from the fire escape and joined the looking up crowd on the sidewalk.

Prince Hope started in writing his script, then informed his people he wanted to go on air.

"People of the United States of America. This is Prince Hope, minister of (unintelligible). I bring you an on the spot report from Minneapolis, Minnesota, sponsored by Really Big Red Trucks."

He told about Korey's climb up "Mount Foshay," once the highest point in Minnesota.

He gave the history of the Foshay Tower that he had found on the plaque in front of the building.

Then he began to read from the CRUSHER leaflet.

"The Pres'dent is actually nothing but a little fucking baby sitting in a rose garden surrounded by people who change his dirty diapers. ..."

Hope turned his face quickly after saying this line and some might say a ghost of a smile escaped before he could force it back into its room.

Hope paused, took a deep breath.

"And that of course is a bold distortion of the truth, a lie meant to (inaudible) ..."

Hope read through the entire leaflet, saying how Korey was climbing, even to his possible death, "to bring attention to the current trial of Evey and Blake, who have attempted to dismantle just one killing machine, which took food out of the mouth of a needy woman with three children."

After each paragraph Hope looked down and then slowly up to begin again.

He had positioned himself so that on the screens all over the country everywhere, over his right shoulder everyone saw Korey climbing the building.

At The 12th Floor Korey pressed himself, his whole body, into the window, along with the side of his face, smooshed. Slowly, carefully, still paying absolute attention to his every breath and move and thought — he still had enough energy, enough absolute fright to be able to keep going — keeping his face firmly planted against the window, he turned his face, smashing his nose, so that he was now looking inside.

There was this face.

Right there, right on the other side of the pane, so close, right there, but this person was safe. Smiling. Smiling Wide.

So many large teeth. A scary shade of white.

A woman with red lipstick, party dress, pert black hair, a tattoo somewhere but he couldn't see where, silver show dog ear rings.

She held up her drink to salute Korey and his smooshed snot nose, his pissed pants, his face scrapes, jammed toe, swollen knee, bleeding fingertips.

Behind her were more people, happy, in suits, ties loosened, maybe this was FRIDAY. Maybe this was just The 15th Floor.

Korey heard some of what they were saying, or singing, mostly an unintelligible mumble.

He looked mostly at the window, so marvelous, so locked, so not able to be opened. He saw it needed cleaning. From the sidewalk you wouldn't see this, water marks, bird crap, bugs.

He didn't want to, but he pulled his head from the window just inches to see the reflection of what was behind him. He saw other buildings, blue sky, clouds, a plane, people in the other building in offices doing their regular things.

And then it became loud and windy.

A sea gull smashed against a window and fell to the ledge dead at Korey's feet.

So loud.

In the reflection Korey now saw a helicopter, sitting in the air, pointed right at him.

He clutched with his fingertips and with his face and his dick and with his toes.

The helicopter swiveled and the camera man filmed Korey as the helicopter blades worked to sweep him to his death on the sidewalk below. The camera man moved to put the reporter on air, then back to Korey.

Korey sweat and he swore as the windows filled with the people in the loosened dresses and ties holding the drinks in the plastic glasses, pointing, waving now as the camera looked their way, unaffected by the windstorm, posing next to Korey's frightened face. A whoosh took him and he caught himself again by sure luck and the partyers noticed it and everyone yipped and yelled and pointed and posed even more.

Korey let go.

He bent at the knees and with his feet cramped sideways on the window ledge, which were not as wide as the other ledges. He grabbed his knees as the helicopter turned and was gone.

He looked down.

He saw all the people, some looking up, shielding their eyes to see, some just standing there, some walking past, annoyed all these people were in their way, all the flashing lights and now heard the sirens continually blowing, wavering, like a London bus trying to get through impossible traffic.

Korey's stomach turned over, the bottom forced up and the top rolled down.

He erupted.

Mt. Korey.

Once. Twice. Again.

The sludge sat in glops on the little ledge and it fell, the three eruptions, each a separate entity, fell down toward the people, who kept looking up. The crud spread out over a wider area as it picked up speed and approached its destination.

It hit as suddenly and violently as a night raid on a suspect's home.

Smacked in the face, knocked backward, forced to knees.

"Ooooh."

"Ewwwww!"

People ran from it, but boom-boom, the next two slime waves hit with viscus lack of empathy and knocked down the rich and the poor, the beautiful and the ugly, faces rubbed sidewalk, knees cracked on cement.

And then it sat there, on the sidewalk.

"He puked," someone said and someone who could have been a reporter wrote it down.

He felt better. He was renewed and fresh and vigorous, like a personality disorder finally confronted if not overcome and ready to keep going with his life, such as it was.

"Woah," said Washington as he backed away, into the street.

Evey and Blake had long since been returned to their cells after a day in court. Used to the routine, almost like having a job and normal life, after getting back they hurried to take a shower, eat, talk to those around them in the different cells, the guards, telling about the day in court, listening to what had happened back here during the day, watching a little TV, eating that delicious Snickers they had been saving, hid under the toothpaste in the crevice between the thin green mattress and the grey steel frame.

And for once, thought Korey, he had done something right.

He had anticipated not being able to make it up the tower in one day.

He so looked forward to being able to sleep, not so much hanging and thinking about falling all night long.

He searched for a spot, not near a window, maybe right under a ledge where he would be invisible sort of, and would have some shelter from rain. Taking his time, as he always tried to do, except for the insane time a few hours ago when he had way too much confidence, he let his backpack down off one shoulder and reached inside for his stretchy rope, his pitons, and his hammer.

He found a way to hold to the ledge with one hand while inserting the pitons — which were really just screwdrivers with holes in the end that he found in the tool room in the underground — into a crevice between the ledge and wall and beating them in tight.

He was losing his light except for the old Grain Belt neon sign on the top of the building across the street. Next he pulled from his bag of tricks his favorite Viet Cong hammock, marked with a big VC on the bottom.

Whispering to himself that slow is smooth and smooth is fast, Korey attached the hammock rings to the clip-ons at the ends of the short stretchy rope that he did not know the real name of, got his legs in, his butt down and taking a giant deep breath, let himself down and trusted in the pink and black screwdrivers and the stretchy rope and the red, blue and yellow Viet Cong hammock as if his life depended on them.

He set himself down soft, still touching the wall, feeling the weave of the hammock on his body, almost relaxing.

Keeping one hand in touch with the precious wall, Korey lay on his back. He looked up and saw lights in the buildings around him and faces and people watching him sleep. He saw a plane cross the sky and he heard honks down below, and a siren. He thought of falling and he stopped that thought about halfway and thought of baseball and a girl and sang himself a song inside his head and he fucking slept.

"Hello, Korey, come in, Korey."

Somewhere the walkie-talkie was still on. He felt his backpack with his toes. He let it be.

"Is this on?

"Korey? Fucking answer me, Korey.

"Hey, sorry.

"Korey?"

Korey lay with his eyes closed, feeling the hammock on his elbows, gently swaying. He felt a breeze and stuck his head farther inside his hoodie, thinking he wouldn't get up until he heard Washington moving around.

He heard a honk and his eyes just opened, he didn't want them to. He peeked up over the hammock and saw a building, people in suits standing at windows holding their coffee and watching him.

Oh, shit.

He yawned and reached for the Pepsi he had planned to be his caffeine for the morning. It foamed and he just let it, licked the top and chugged it back, coughing, careful not to move around and have one of the screwdrivers let loose and die.

He yawned again and stretched.

He was so sore, his legs, his arms, and oh, god, his neck. Even his toes and his butt were so sore.

Korey couldn't just pop up. He knew that. He heard Washington in the walkie-talkie, but he couldn't reach it. He knew he had to start thinking just as soon as the Pepsi started to work.

He had to think about exactly what to do and in what order to get him from swinging in the hammock to standing, *oh God*, on the side of a building on the who knows what floor and he was going to die today unless he woke up right now and got all pumped again and alert and scared and into it. *Goddamnit.* He cursed himself for this idea.

The fire escape was there. He didn't know if it like touched each floor he was so fucking sore. Nope. He was not going to walk down and face all those people down there like that. If they did see him it'd be with his screaming face headed right down on top of 'em. He stretched his fists to the sky and yawned and remembered the Snickers he had brought. And he smiled.

Down below, as Korey reached The 16th Floor and the person in the purple hair changed the tally on the chalkboard, a man dressed as Superman walked into the middle of the crowd.

"No," he said to Washington, who was reaching for him to say this building is taken, man, pointing to his own chest where it said: Capt. America.

His suit was all red, white and blue with a face mask, all that shit. And a yellow ribbon pin or some shit.

"I'll get him," the man turned to the two policemen standing there.

One of the cops shrugged his shoulders.

"Knock yerself out."

The man tapped his knuckles on the red, white and blue helmet he wore.

"Those stupid cops don't even know there is a fire escape," Capt. America said slyly to Washington. "I don't need it. Faster my way."

The man, Capt. America, turned to the chamber group playing to collect money for The Ronald McDonald House.

"If you please?"

They picked up their shit, coffee lattes, turned their metal chairs around and one nodded to Capt. America when they were ready.

He bounded up to the building, waved big to the crowd, said something about democracy that almost nobody could hear because of all the city noise and turned to climb up the building after Korey.

The chamber group played *The William Tell Overture*, some were thinking.

"Oh, yeah," said Washington, "I've heard that, on cartoons."

A young woman standing next to him said, "With that big fighter that Bugs Bunny boxes, Crusher."

"Nah, I don't think so," said Washington.

"Never heard of him."

The young woman argued with Washington for a while that it was definitely a thing.

Way up there Korey heard the music and he could see something down there that wasn't there before. A bug on the wall? How could he see a bug on the wall? Unless because of the altitude the Pepsi gave him powers. That would be cool.

He turned to begin again and his foot slipped. Maybe his hands and other foot weren't quite where they should be. Maybe he had taken a couple of holds for granted because he was weary, but he slipped.

And because that put more weight on his hands and his other foot, they could not hold either.

So he fell.

Or so he thought.

He dropped and his life flashed like it does, so quickly, and his heart jumped and all those cliché things that happen, they do happen.

He hit the ledge right below him that he had forgotten was there and he would have kept falling past that if he had not had the good fortune that his hands somehow knew to grab onto whatever they could without him having to think about it because they were going to die too.

He held on and put his forehead against the building and the building seemed to sway and he was falling backward, with the building. He was forcing the building to fall and he would fall on his back and the building would be on top of him.

Korey took a deep breath, let it out slowly. That felt good and he did it again. He tried it a third time and it wasn't as good as the first two, so that was enough.

During a break in their trial, Evey and Blake were left alone for a while in the lunch room. They saw on the TV on the wall where the camera showed the chalkboard and the smiling person who had made it her job to mark each floor of Korey's Climb, along with a nice chalk drawing she had made of CRUSHER climbing the Foshay Tower.

The camera then looked straight up and the reporter pointed out the "new entrant in the race to the top," along with Korey way up there.

Now that it had become a race of sorts, more attention seemed to be focused on the little area where Washington was keeping vigil. So Washington kind of had to keep moving around and giving dirty looks and getting pissed at people who stood in front of him because he was basically incognito. Through all of this moving and getting annoyed he was able to contact Korey once in awhile by walkie-talkie and tell him what was happening and who was pissing him off.

The sidewalk was getting crammed and the cars on the street sometimes even stopped right there, not even bothering to keep moving.

The chamber group smiled at each other as they were getting some donations into the big floppy hat and they played louder: dun, dun, dun, dun, dundadundundun.

Korey got excited. Now he couldn't stop himself from looking down about every ten seconds. The looking down was drawing his attention away from the climbing and the not falling and which end was up and down.

He closed his eyes, rested his forehead against the limestone and tried to contact The Woo, to give him strength, guidance, hope. He said those words in his head and waited. Nothing.

He looked up to see what he had coming next, found his holds and pushed off, slowly. He moved his hip a little to feel the knife. He would fight the guy behind him when he got up here.

At The 17th Floor the windows were filled with orange signs: Marry Me Korey, Go CRUSHER!

They did not hate him on this floor. They almost liked him and that was a weird feeling and in a way it made it harder than if they were yelling and pointing fingers.

Korey looked down and could see the red, white and blue

of the person following him, coming fast, who was not a bug anymore.

At The 17th Floor when Korey got to the window, with his face as usual needing to be pressed right against the window, he saw breasts, big beautiful breasts, with silver dollar pancake nipples, pressed against the other side, and a pretty woman holding up her shirt and smiling and licking her lip.

And in the next window a guy was holding up his shirt.

Then behind the girl and the guy came a roomful of guys with their shirts up.

Korey looked down and wondered what sorts of trials red, white and blue guy was suffering. He was too fast. Korey looked up and it seemed like he had forever to go yet. He could see where the building maybe ended and kind of see the antenna at the very top, kind of.

At The 20th Floor mark it was getting cold.

Korey thought he saw snow flurries though he could not really look around. To see the snow it would have to fall right between the one inch between his nose and the building.

It *is* Minnesota, he said to himself. I just love this town.

He reached the window.

There stood Alexa, Trevor or Brad or Brent, and Marv, all wearing their suits, all in a line.

Brad or Brent or Trevor held out an open hand and Korey's missing tooth.

Thanks, *Brad*, thought Korey, now that was all he was going to think about. His tongue found the open space.

He supposed what they wanted to tell him was, was that after this is over, he will be theirs.

Not really, he thought.

He had options.

Meanwhile, at the base of the HOLLYWOOD sign … Alice, Charlie, Frida, and Ike were having some trouble, with their broadcast, having enough food, talking only to each other, their human waste disposal system, being bored out of their minds and mostly not knowing if anyone was hearing them. They had nobody to ask.

They didn't know that Rachel and Jorge had Evey's phone.

Their days were spent in a split-personality world of hiding at the base of the sign and also trying to get the world to hear them through their broadcasts. They had to walk to the convenience store almost five miles away, hitchhiking was kind of forbidden, and their latrine was starting to really stink.

They had no idea that Marv, Alexa and Brad or Trevor or Brent, in addition to watching Korey climb were searching frantically for the clandestine radio show "The Americans," that was sweeping the nation, even though they thought they were calling it "Live From Hollywood."

"Whazzuuup?" said Alice.

"I thought we were calling the show "Live From Hollywood."

"It's 'The Americans,' a segment of *Live From Hollywood*," said Frida.

"It's complicated," said Alice.

"Yep," said Frida.

"What's up?" said Alice.

"Oh, Charlie's trippin'," said Frida, "something not workin'."

"You got to give him snaps for even trying," said Alice.

"Psyche," said Frida, "I was just gonna say that.

"Hey," she said to Ike, "stylin'."

Ike was wearing a Baywatch T-shirt he'd found on the rack on a recent trip to the convenience store.

"Phat," said Alice.

"We need to dip on outa here," said Ike.

"No duh," said Alice.

"What's for breakfast?" asked Frida.

"Yer gonna have to guess," said Ike.

"So, so mysterious," said Frida in her Homer Simpson voice.

"I feel like I'm in a friggin' '90s sitcom," said Charlie, sitting right there, fiddling with the equipment. "You guys are going crazy, whacked," he used air quotes.

"I can't get this to work," he added.

"Word," said Ike. "What the 4-1-1? Take a chill pill."

"If this doesn't stop — *right now* — I'm leaving," Charlie stood up.

Each one of them zipped their lips and locked them, threw away the key.

Korey, crawling like a bug, was having problems with orientation at The 27th Floor. Maybe it was vertigo, but at times it felt like he was crawling on flat ground and sometimes like he was crawling down. And he was having dizzy spells.

Also, the walkie-talkie not working, out of power. And as far as he knew there were no extra batteries, at least that he could feel inside the backpack.

And Capt. America was gonna catch him if he didn't really pick it up.

Korey reached the ledge of The 27th Floor and sat with his legs dangling.

And he was so surprised.

For the first time— except The Time Of Insanity when he made like five floors in an hour way down there — he felt calm, at ease like he belonged there and he had this.

Between his knees he watched Capt. America catching his different holds, peeking up, and pushing up, up.

Jorge and Rachel sat on the little cement back porch listening to the frogs, both whittling, Jorge the Virgin Mary, Rachel a gun.

They listened to the Twins game and also by Evey's phone to Prince Hope … and news coverage of The Trial and The Climb.

Hope did not seem happy with the coverage Evey, Blake and Korey were getting. But he was one of the ones who had made that happen. I am about ready to call WTF on PH. They say psychopaths rule us. Do you think that's true? I don't think that's true. They are basically good people and very smart and very able to handle life, conversations, meetings, dinner parties. I couldn't do all that. But I don't understand how they can kill and not seem to care and to lie. I just couldn't do that. But they laugh. They tell jokes. They look just like us. WTF?

"It is not THE TRIAL and THE CLIMB," Prince Hope said.

"They are nothing, less than nothing. You'll see.

"You are to think of them as nothing. Don't think of them at all. See, it's not raining now, play Frisbee. That is fun and enjoyable and people love it and stay in physical condition."

"He sounds like Chairman Meow," said Jorge to nobody exactly.

"What pawpaw?" said Rachel.

"Nothing mija. Little joke with your grandma."

"Is she here?" said Rachel.

"Yes."

"Say hello for me."

"She says brush your teeth, and you're getting so big," said Jorge.

Rachel smiled wide and whittled harder than ever.

Korey waited and watched the buzz around him build. He was the middle of the hive, the king bee. It was his ballgame, like it had been on the bridge that night. But this time he was not going to survive to fight another day. This was gonna be pretty much it. There were police all over down below and probably up on the roof, too, and in helicopters and buildings all around, and this guy was chasing him, right up the freeking building, probly a cop.

Korey looked up behind him to see what was happening in the window and to judge how far he had still to go. He was so fucking tired. He decided to wait. He pulled out his long knife and set it by him on the ledge and swung his feet like he was on the playground.

Korey put his head back and yelled.

"Aaaaah! Fuuuuuck it!

"Fuck it! Fuck it! Fuuuuucck iiiiit!"

He waited, listened for the echo.

He closed his eyes.

He breathed deep, let it out, again, again, preparing to die.

He felt the Woo. *The Woooo*. He could fucking feel it.

He felt it in his chest and his arms and his legs, exactly like he sensed it in the underground during their vision quest.

Sitting on the edge of her bed in her cell, her feet flat on the floor, her hands folded in her lap, Josephine Custer smiled with her eyes closed. She smelled the sage and she thought of the movie Dances With Wolves, no, the other one, Braveheart, nope ... Thunderheart, and she rode a horse in battle, whooping, raising her tomahawk. She heard the keys and the doors and the shouts and the noise of the prison, but she was not there. A guard looked in through the narrow vertical window and saw her sitting in the middle of her bed, but she was not there. She was riding.

She felt the muscles and the bones of her horse as she bounded over the rough prairie ground. Her stomach leaped as they shot up a little hill to its crest and kept going, jumping, heading toward the enemy, with renewed vigor and force and noise, and anger. She tilted her head back and howled in her vision and in her cell and then she leaned forward on her horse, steel and thunder and lightening bolts and timberwolves in her eyes, Marsha-Marsha-Marsha, The Beautiful Indian Maiden Heroine, Josephine Custer, muscles taught and bulging, blood surging, singing her death song, belting it out, full-blast.

Exhausted, Evey closed her eyes and took a deep breath, held it, letting everything come to her, all thoughts all feelings, all smells, all sounds.

The scowl left her forehead and she grinned wide, mostly inside her heart, keeping it to herself. She stretched her neck this way and that like she had seen ballplayers do. It helped.

She touched Blake's hand. He was listening so intently to what was being said. He nodded to her and looked back to the room.

Evey let her head fall back and closed her eyes.

She thought of Jorge and Maria and the stories they told, and about this and that, it was hard to concentrate with the talk around her, but what she could find in her mind was a picture of a grandmother and grandfather, a photo, a black and white photo, sitting on a stoop in Mexico, adobe hut, her mother, Maria, sitting nearby in the hard dirt, in her first communion dress, a cracked baby doll in her arm, a skinny grey dog sitting nearby, and they are eating some sort of tortilla on this festive occasion, all staring hard into the camera, not used to posing for photos.

Actually, sitting outside by himself on break, closed his eyes and felt himself sitting next to Korey on The 27th Floor downtown.

Frida, taking a walk by herself in the scrub and brush around HOLLYWOOD, decided to sit. She crossed her legs and meditated. It took awhile. She had not had time for this for so long, but within twenty minutes she joined with the others. She had no idea. Nobody had any idea.

In his office, with the window open, Prince Hope turned away from his computer, turned back and closed it, turned back again and shut it off. He looked out at Korey, now so high up here, just sitting, like a mountain goat, so used to the setting. Hope leaned back, folded his hands behind his head and closed his eyes.

The red head inched closer.

Korey stood, squatted slowly again to pick up the knife and moved to the far end of the ledge.

Closer.

Another helicopter appeared, now another. Every window in the two, three buildings, oh, one more behind him, filled with people watching.

Rachel watched on Evey's phone as Capt. America drew within one floor of Korey The CRUSHER. She huddled against the house, put her knees up and pulled a piece of sweet grass to chew because she had seen it done by others.

Korey walked over to help him up and then backed off, not cool, he decided.

Finally, breathing hard, his suit drenched with sweat, his knees and elbows torn and bleeding, Capt. America pulled himself and stood. He put up both arms like Rocky and waved to all the buildings around.

"You made some good goddamn time," said Korey.

Capt. America seemed to have no time for small talk. He reached behind and pulled his pistol.

"Are you a cop?" said Korey.

"You arrestin' me? What we got goin' on here?"

"Well, I'm not a cop," said Capt. America.

"It says Captain America on your head and on your chest. I just saw that," said Korey.

"Yes, of course," said the guy.

"I'm just a citizen doing his duty."

"Your duty?

"Yer fuckin' stupid for one thing," said Korey.

He stepped forward two steps and Capt. America took a two-handed, bent knee stance.

"You brought a gun to a knife fight," said Korey.

"Whatever you fuckin' do, don't look up."

"Up? Why?" said Capt. America, looking down, over his outstretched arm.

Korey swiped the knife and cut his hand and wrist. The gun bounced off the building and ricocheted back, up over Capt. America's head. He reached for it, but missed, it happened so fast. The pistol fell. They watched it drifting down, down, the pop, it landed and fired.

"Didn't hit nobody," said Korey, "probly."

He advanced on Capt. America with the long Ka-Bar.

"Where'd you get that knife?" said Capt. America. "That's a good knife."

"This is a war, Zeke," said Korey, "or haven't you heard?"

Capt. America began to look concerned, holding his hands out toward Korey, looking around, behind him.

"So," said Korey.

"How's this gonna go?"

"What do you mean?"

"I mean … am I gonna cut you up and toss you overboard for bait for all those sharks at the bottom, or are you gonna take the fire escape, are you gonna jump, or are you gonna crawl back down?"

"I'm not taking the fire escape," said Capt. America.

"Okay," said Korey.

"Then that leaves Door Number One or Door Number Three, or Number Four."

He stepped closer and really he could give a shit. If he had to kill Capt. America right there on TV so be it. It might have shown in his eyes.

Capt. America put one leg down off the ledge, then another.

"You're a good climber," said Korey.

"Thanks. You, too."

He sure is fucking fast, thought Korey as he watched Capt. America make it down three stories in no time, dragging blood all the way.

Korey waved to the people and the cameras. He held up his knife, with the blood on it.

That's not good, thought Rachel, just sayin', showing the bloody knife like that.

Korey put the knife away, checked again on Capt. America's progress and decided to kick it in the ass and try to make it to the top yet today. He was pretty sure if he stayed the night someone would shoot him down now.

With five floors to go, but not really knowing that exactly, feeling kind of good after winning the fight, and looking like a pirate to Rachel, Korey took off, actually jumping up to his first foothold.

Prince Hope opened his eyes, watched Korey for a while, then turned again to his computer.

Evey and Blake were led out of the courtroom for the day at about the same time that Frida got up to head back to the bunker for something to eat, probly not much, a cigarette, and another night of radio theater that was fun, but was it doing anything, that's the thing.

Hope went right to CraigsList.

"Come in, Korey," said Washington into his walkie.

"Nice goin' with the fight, but, yeah, not sure how that's all gonna play, the blood, and stuff, well, call back when you can."

It took Korey at least two hours of full-out climbing and yet not going too fast and then fucking falling to make the top fucking floor.

He grabbed hold with both hands and pushed out a little to look down and wave with one hand. From what he could tell nobody down there did nothing. He looked at the people in all the windows and they just kinda watched him.

Well, he knew when he climbed over this last big ledge there would be a big reception and not with streamers and whistles and party hats.

He thought about it. What you're thinking.

Yeah, he waited a bit and considered the possibilities.

It might be cool, for about two and one-half seconds, but shit. The reason he did this was to draw attention to the trial, not really to him, and he didn't know if he did that, but it was s'posed to with the press release leaflets if Washington remembered to even hand 'em out.

Korey pulled himself up over to the top, the one leg over, then the next, oh, man, his legs were hurtin'.

He could see the whole top and all there was, was a big antenna and a door like a tornado shelter door, a door like you see on movies on the top of buildings where eventually somebody comes storming out, late for some fucking reason, either they forgot or were waiting for someone else to use the restroom, didn't know the top was this close or that far up, they got lost or some fucking thing, draws a gun and either shoots or rushes and tackles the guy up there because of whatever the fuck he's doin' up there.

Jorge talked to Frida in Hollywood, didn't know he could, Rachel had touched something and it dialed up Frida.

He was catching her up on all that was happening.

And especially that yes, they heard their radio theater on the radio right in their kitchen.

Kind of fuzzy, he said, but you're way out in California, right?

He told her where to go to see The Climb on their phone.

"Oh, yeah, there it is. Cool. He's holding the big antenna thing."

"Hey!" Charlie yelled so Jorge could hear him way in Minnesota.

"Have him keep doing that!" said Charlie.

"Actually, have him keep doing that," said Frida.

"How could that help?" said Jorge.

"Dunno, but Charlie says it does."

It was windy up there, so Korey held the antenna to keep from blowing away. It would be not cool if he was way on top and all of a sudden he is swooped up over the edge and splat it's over after all of that.

Like whatever.

He made his way to the edge to hoist himself up to look over.

He walked around up there.

What now? The thought crossed his mind.

He sat down to rest and put his head back against the wall, closed his eyes, listened to the seagulls and the helicopters and the door squeaking open.

Korey shot up to stand, pulled his knife as Alexa, Brad or Trevor or Brent, and Marv rushed out of the door and headed his way, guns pulled and pointing.

Prince Hope closed out of Craigslist and turned to the window. He checked his watch, got up to check over here, over there, saw something that made him sit down to watch.

Prince Hope could not see. Nobody in any of the buildings could see. Nobody anywhere, except whoever was in the two helicopters hovering could see what was happening up on that roof.

Korey faced off with the three very familiar C.I.A. agents, wearing their black and white uniforms, sunglasses, and yellow ribbon pins and American flag cuff links.

"Oh, Korey. Didn't anyone tell you? You're the unpopular one … again. You brought a knife to a …," said Brad.

"You little git," said Korey, tossing his knife to a downward ripping and gouging position.

At that they spread out, Marv focused on him while Alexa and Brad or Trevor flanked.

They waited at their familiar table for the jury to file in.

The judge appeared.

Someone's knee bumped something wooden and whispered "sorry."

And for a few seconds all was quiet as everyone stared at the judge arranging busily some papers.

The judge looked up.

"The jury has come to a decision?"

"Yes, your honor."

Just like on TV, the guard got the piece of paper from the jury foreman and handed it to the judge then returned to his wall.

The judge asked everyone to be quiet and to be quiet after the verdict is read.

Blake reached out to hold Evey's hand. Evey also held the hand of their attorney.

Blake whispered to Evey, "Deus ex machina," and she said what? with her eyebrows and he said, "whatever will be, will be, that one song you like," and she said, no, I don't think so by shaking her head and looking back at the judge and she dug her fingernail into either Blake's finger or her attorney's, she knew she had but she immediately forgot which one and who cares now anyway.

Nobody on that roof saw that coming.

It hung and it moved toward them, pulled by the little plane way up there apparently though the rope could nigh have been invisible. It soared a little, then headed straight down like a hawk with a mouse in its sights.

Silently the orange hang glider swooped in low, picking up speed, claws down.

Korey felt something smack him hard in his legs as if he had been shot and knock the knife from his hand. He lifted up away from the stunned guns, still pointed up at him, following his ascent, like parents at the MOA, pointing at their kids on the roller coaster, with fingers usually, not guns.

One member of "Harley's Tandem Hang Gliding Rescue Teams, Get Your Cat Out Of The Tree Or Your Dog Off The Roof, Three Locations In The Twin Cities," held Korey firmly on the bar while the other piloted as they removed Korey from the building top as a mother bird taking a baby from a nest that had become too dangerous.

Korey's new captors spoke not a word as they soared, following the river.

"Woah," said Korey, smiling, looking all around.

***

Rachel sat up straight on Roswell and shot her fists into the air.

Jorge looked up at her from the ground as they returned from their walk.

He smiled and also wondered, WTF? How could this happen? Where was the trap? They are fooling them somehow, watch it, my Evey.

Evey stood and turned and squeezed Blake. They both hugged their attorney. Evey ran around the courtroom, shaking everyone's hands, the judge, the jury, the prosecuting attorney, the people in the crowd who she had no idea who they were but they had been sitting there for months, same seats.

She fell into her familiar chair at the table, bowed her head and put her hands over her face.

The Pres'dent watched on the TV, eating his cereal at his desk, as Korey was rescued.

And he thought to himself, WTF?

On the sidewalk everybody looked up like hairless chicks waiting to be fed and nobody saw anything except by the TVs everywhere.

As Korey was whisked away some cheered, some just walked away, some thought it was all staged, part of a promotion for cereal or red trucks.

Washington tried the walkie again, rushed around, found at least most of his shit and ran. As he sprinted, his shirt tail streaming like a kite, he thought. He knew he did not know why he was running or where, but to be running felt good, and so he did.

In HOLLYWOOD they jumped around and hugged after having just heard on the phone about the trial and now Korey. Oh my god!

"Gooo KO-Rey, go KO-rey."

Jorge and Rachel high-fived and Evey and Blake were beaming in the back of the black van as they and the guards listened to the action on the radio.

Prince Hope turned back to his computer and his legal pad and wrote out his story where he would denounce the hooligan and call for citizens to assist in his capture and inevitable execution.

Josephine Custer, sitting on her bed, now with her back against the wall, breathed deep, opened her eyes and smiled.

QUOTE REMOVED BY ORDER OF DHS, UNITED STATES
DEPARTMENT OF HOMELAND SECURITY. [DHS US2FA]

I am poor and naked,
but I am the chief of the nation.
We do not want riches
but we do want to train our children right.
Riches would do us no good.
We could not take them with us
to the other world.
We do not want riches.
We want peace and love.
— Red Cloud, *Oglala Lakota Sioux*

Humankind has not woven the web of life. We are
but one thread within it. Whatever we do to the web,
we do to ourselves. All things are bound together.
All things connect. ... When you know who you
are; when your mission is clear and you burn with
the inner fire of unbreakable will; no cold can touch
your heart; no deluge can dampen your purpose.
You know that you are alive.
— Chief Seattle

A very great vision is needed and the man who
has it must follow it as the eagle seeks the deepest
blue of the sky.
— Crazy Horse, *Oglala Lakota Sioux*

TWENTY-SEVEN

Frida was up first.

The sun was in her eyes even though she slept with her arm across her face just for that reason.

She rolled over and saw the other sleeping bags arranged back to back, foot to foot, head to head in the space inside the sandbags that had been their home for how many months.

She slowly climbed out of her bag, worked to get the cook stove going and start the coffee. She rubbed her eyes and yawned big, looking down at the highway that always buzzed but you didn't really hear it anymore. She went back to the latrine, behind the second "L," squatted into the cement block, smoked a cigarette. Down below a car was stopped. She didn't remember seeing it before.

"Hey."

Somebody else was waking up.

"Time is it?" somebody said too loud because that's what you do when you are in that goofy insane waking up mood.

"Six ... thirty ... seven," said Frida.

That person groaned and crunched up inside their bag.

The guy with the car was now standing in front of the open hood, hands on hips, now folded behind head, now head folded back searching for answers in the cloudless sky, like he had hoped to have discovered a new planet, but this wasn't it.

Frida shoved her weapon inside the back of her pants and put one leg over the sandbags.

"Shit. I'm goin' down," she announced, taking a longing look at the not-ready yet coffee.

That's what they did when somebody stalled in the stretch below them. See what they could do. Sometimes they got cigarettes in return but they told themselves that was not the reason. And they didn't really want a bunch of people hanging around and then one of them looks up and says, hey, what is that up there? You know?

She didn't hear any grunt of acknowledgment but that didn't mean they didn't hear her. She entered the steep descent, with a sort of sideways canter. She began to sweat. Down below it was really hot already, out of the shadow of the sign and the hill.

They always came down, not right from the sign, but from the side, to confuse anyone wondering where they had just appeared from.

"Oh, I'm just parked a ways away," said Frida, "out lookin' for arrowheads, first time out west, ya know, just saw ya over here, what seems to be the problem?" she said her regular lines, perhaps a bit too dryly, she'd work on that.

The man moved suddenly, stepped back and reached quickly into his pocket? ... *for something.*

Frida, foggy without her coffee, did not draw her weapon, just looked at him, puzzled, her mind gears whirring, trying to catch hold of anything.

At the "pop-pop-pop ... pop," everybody was up, out of the sleeping bags, kneeling, standing, looking down at the highway where Frida lay on her back.

"What the fuck!" Charlie grabbed his rifle, leaped the barricade and skidded to a stop, falling on his side, throwing up dust. He stretched out there watching as a flurry of vehicles squealed, careened in at all angles where Frida lay not moving.

Alice watched with binoculars.

There were California state patrol, CHIPS, sirens blaring, lights flashing, officers scrambled, behind vehicles, aiming weapons up the hill.

Charlie fought to get over their front wall as little puffs flew up all around him.

Now a helicopter landed on the highway and they could see roadblocks set up on both sides of the median.

Charlie, Ike and Alice hurried to get loaded, find everything and talk to each other to ask what was going on?

"Why's she *down* there? Alone!" said Ike.

"I *think* I heard her," said Alice, "I don't know!"

"God-dammit!" shouted Charlie.

Without aiming he fired at the cars, now including a National Guard troop carrier.

The soldiers poured out of the truck and spread across the lower edge of the hill.

Ike leaped to cover their rear as they heard vehicle doors and shouts up above.

"Get down, down," Charlie waved his hand at Ike, because where he had planted himself left him open to fire from below.

They looked up at the sound of strange clunks as holes appeared in all the letters of the sign. The sandbags were continually thumped as if a whole office of manual typewriters were going full-blast.

From above, a film shown on the evening news, a camera shot from a helicopter displayed how the circle had now been drawn around the HOLLYWOOD sign and the bunker at the foot of the "H."

Some news reporters were speculating that the group was hippies from the '60s who had never been found.

The three, Alice, Ike, Charlie fired their automatic AR-15s, their handguns as fast and furiously as they could, all around the circle as it advanced slowly toward them, closing, smaller circle, smaller.

First Ike was hit, in the thigh, then a round went right through Alice's shoulder. She switched to shooting right-handed.

From the front, straight up the hill, climbed a mixture of highway patrol, LAPD, National Guard and L.A. County sheriff's office, and on the top and flanks the three remaining CRUSHERS fought regular Army troops.

Flashing lights lined all sides of the highway, and crowds gathered in the neighborhoods as close as they could get to the freeway, on bridges, ramps. Children found a way to get through to sit in the tall grass to watch. Colorful blankets sprang up on the hillsides above the freeway and people sat on five-gallon buckets to play drums and guitar and make a little money. Young boys in no shirts perched on rooftops like city goats.

A young boy reported later that he watched through his birthday binoculars as "the guy in the black hair got shot through the mouth."

He laughed and smiled and the news reporter laughed and smiled when the boy said, "I think I even got blood on me, I looked, there was a lot."

The shooting eventually died down, to a few pops, then everyone realized it was over, and they moved closer a few steps, over the guard railing, onto the freeway concrete, shuffling down the exit ramp a bit closer as the cops seemed to relax.

For a couple of hours the freeway remained closed as ambulances without sirens or lights pulled up, and police cars had to be moved to make room. All the cops and soldiers headed to the bunker and stayed there for a long while in a big bunch as the news copters tried for the money shot.

At the end of the afternoon all that was left were the final ambulance and Frida's body on the side, and all the kids and others waiting to run up the hill.

Somebody said someone found some sunglasses and somebody found a knife with blood.

"That's a Ka-Bar," said an older man to the kid.

"We had those in 'Nam.

"Damn good knives."

QUOTE REMOVED BY ORDER OF DHS, UNITED STATES
DEPARTMENT OF HOMELAND SECURITY. [DHS US2FA]

The song tells how, as I sing, I go through the air to a holy place where Yusun will give me power to do wonderful things. I am surrounded by little clouds, and as I go through the air I change, becoming spirit only.

— Geronimo, *Apache*

TWENTY-EIGHT

The rest of the summer flew by and before you knew it, it was that day again.

"Good morning."

The sign over the front door said, "Welcome To Geronimo's Day!"

The Friendly Face Facility staff wore shorts, and feathers and headbands and moccasins, beads, dream catcher necklaces and ear rings, and bright orange T-shirts with CRUSHER in bold white letters across the front.

It was a carnival with games set up in the hallways and the classrooms, and the big event was the wrestling match with a real ring set up in the small gym.

"Holy," said Evey when she saw Mike Braxton.

"What am I doing here?" he said.

"My son goes here," he said as a smiling young man walked up to him and asked for more cards.

"You might have to sign some autographs," said Braxton.

He showed Evey the CRUSHER playing cards.

"I had to make 'em, but I never did anything with them, so I brought them today."

"You look different," said Evey.

"I finally did something Lara asked me to do a long time ago. Maybe that's it."

"No," she said as Blake came over.

Evey and Blake left Braxton, to wander the halls and see the different games.

The smell of sage invisibly filled the halls.

"Oh, sure."

They were asked a few times to sign the CRUSHER playing cards. Evey was the Queen of Hearts, Blake the Six of Clubs.

They saw two young men wearing singlets that said "Geronimo," and "Bad Guy."

Evey and Blake laughed with clients and staff members they knew.

"Oh, look at that!"

They visited their old classrooms, they played the game with the floating yellow ducks, bean bag toss and nerf bowling.

A smiling young man walked right up to them wearing a T-shirt that said "You Don't Have To Have An Extra Y Chromosome To Work Here But It Helps," held out his hand and said it was time to come watch the wrestling.

They sat in the metal folding chairs. The ring was set up on the gym floor with the volleyball set and bunji cords.

The Friendly Face director got into the ring and thanked all the parents and guests for coming. The two wrestlers stepped inside the ring along with a medicine man. He spoke in Ojibwe and lit a pipe, showed it to the four directions.

Braxton appeared next to Evey. He reached across to shake Blake's hand.

"Good guy always wins, right?" said Braxton.

The director stepped back in.

She put a nerf microphone to her mouth and said, "Are you ready to rumble?"

Everyone cheered as the wrestlers took their spots in the same corner and then opposite corners. Some held signs that said "Geronimo," and "Crusher."

Korey sat in an empty seat next to Blake. He leaned forward to wave to Evey, who tried to alert him to Braxton sitting next to her.

"Bear Hug!" someone hollered and Geronimo tried to put Bad Guy into a grip.

"Body Avalanche!"

"Drop Kick!"

"Power Slam!"

Braxton had disappeared.

Korey got up to slide in front of Blake to take Braxton's empty chair next to Evey.

Korey laughed along with the rest and whispered to Evey, asking about the trial. She fired hurried whispered questions about his climb. They knocked fists. Korey reached across to tap-tap with Blake.

Evey smiled and held up her arms, cheering.

"Yaaay!"

"I think it's just fake," said Blake.

Evey smiled up at him and just shook her head.

"Yaaaay, Geronimo!" she yelled.

"You can do it!"

Across the ring, in the middle of the crowd, two familiar faces popped up like whac-a-mole characters. Evey leaned over, smiling, to point at something happening in the ring and saw the look on Korey's face.

"What's the matter?" she said.

"Nothing, I gotta go."

It happened fast and so unexpected, like the auto accident Max talked about so long ago. One moment you are driving along singing, pounding out on the steering wheel "Just Another Brick In The Wall!" and something comes out of your side vision and your day is going in a totally different direction.

Korey, in about the third row, stood. Alexa and Troy or Brent or Brad both pulled their guns and aimed. Evey in an instant made the connection, put up her arms and stood in front of Korey, yelling "NO!" and at the same time, the crowd screamed, thinking it was a gag for the show.

Not many heard the pop, pop-pop-pop as Korey turned and ran as Evey stood for a moment in pose, hands high, blood running down her light jacket and now CRUSHER orange T-shirt exposed as she lay on her back and Blake tried to think of everything at once you were s'posed to do when something like this happens.

So bravely he went to her, knelt over her and with wet face attempted to secure the scene, get the words out.

In the ring, Geronimo pounded the floor and shot up, his hands raised, as he won. The Bad Guy got up quickly and hugged Geronimo and they both stood in the middle of the ring, hands raised together, beaming, all their friends and family cheering.

Evey strained to see from her position flat on her back on the floor.

"Did we win?" she asked Blake.

"Is everyone okay?"

An ambulance silently pulled to the side gym door. Evey was taken out as everyone watched, wondering if it was real or if it was fake.

Blake walked with her, holding her hand, leaning forward, straining to keep up as she said something about Rachel, Jorge, Korey.

QUOTE REMOVED BY ORDER OF DHS, UNITED STATES
DEPARTMENT OF HOMELAND SECURITY. [DHS US2FA]

Well, it's been another long week in Saint Paul,
Minnesota, my home town, at the end of the empire.
— Prince Hope

TWENTY-NINE

Things don't look good.

Raining again today.

But those CRUSHERS.

For me, they keep me going. They have for years. I don't know what I'm gonna do once they're not around. No, I do, I just don't want to think about it.

Just think, there once were these young people who saw all the superhero movies and comics and decided they would make it all real. Me, if I were a superhero wrestler, I'm afraid it would be "Old Guy," but these CRUSHERS, my god, and all the other people I've talked about in this story I've unfolded for you. I see it now how they and Osama bin Laden, The Easter Bunny, The Cherry Tree, if they didn't exist, they'd have to be invented.

I know, right? Huh?

I once thought that at this point I would insert a bunch of stuff about me, pretty much basically because when I was young I always thought a book would be written about me, either by me or by someone else, all the great stuff I had done. But now I see that if a book or a passage like that is to be written about me it will only contain horrible things.

Maybe some things are better left unsaid, understated, subtle nuance, left out totally, like that. I mean, really, who wants to know? What's that about the most important parts of the book are the ones you leave out? I'm not sure about the most important part, but maybe the weirdest. And I'm not sure what good that does. I think I might be an alien. Sometimes I feel like I'm trying to learn how to speak English or at least Human. It's not easy. That's part of it. I mean this enormous head. It does not seem to match the body, in my estimation. *If I were an alien, ya-ba-dabba, ya-ba dabba dibby dum ... all day long I'd ...*

They buried Evey on the little hill, with Geronimo, Jim, Lara, Kaitylyn.

After the ceremony Rachel ran away. Jorge let her go.

Korey showed up, not in disguise, ashamed, hoping to get arrested, hoping to get shot right there and drop into the hole with Evey. Nobody came.

It had been awhile, but I received another note from our prison writer, Bill, from Iowa, home again after escaping by walking away from the mental hospital.

Not sure what he's been up to, but I just hope to myself that he's been taking long cruises with The Callwell Boys and spending long lazy afternoons conversing with the neighborhood Bigfoot clan, making intricate stick formations and gossiping 'bout the townies.

But who knows, who really knows, who can know for sure, for really.

I do love his stories, his letters.

It's just good, for me, to know there is someone out there like Bill.

Someone who is interested, who takes all this fucking shit seriously, who feels it, who is going over it, grinding through the days, and yeah, I guess, suffering through the times. Somebody un-stupid, who has read, and yeah, I guess it would be somebody on the edge, somebody not sure about getting by, and still caring enough.

You would think that one morning he might see his email to the same little group of people and in it he has poured out the daily news and interpretation and he thinks, what the fuck? This is doing absolutely nothing.

I also wonder the same exact thing.

I wish I could do something. I hope these books about Geronimo and CRUSHER will do something, but they won't. They just won't. And I have to somehow fool myself into thinking that they will because the day I realize the truth, well, what is left?

And so it goes, did Vonnegut say that? You know he wrote some cool stuff they say and people told him he was good, but have you tried to read his books? Just saying.

I am just saying.

I'm glad Bill is out there. Somebody has to be smart and

tough and reading and drinking all day and living alone in a trailer and chopping wood and walking the dogs and making homemade chili and giving a shit.

And then getting up and doing it again the next day.

There just has to be.

Look around you and if that's all there is, if these people are all there are, if Bill is not there.

Well, then what the fuck?

I know, right?

Geoffrey,

Mailed you another of these Jon Rappoport pieces on medicine in the USA. He writes about sundry, is a philosopher, age 80, but what I enjoy from him is medicine in the USA.

My problem is but authority, which makes me asthmatic.

Rather than be schizoid, to respect our lying chickenshit authority.

The dog walks go forth. This morning before spying Kelly and Jazz and Bo at the fork Mike was telling me what he had been reading or seeing on the Web was it. About it has become less certain human beings developed first in Africa. I told him I know this. Oh, you know about this? Mike, from the sixties. And lately it has become less certain (hell, past coupe decades). Oh, you know about this! Mike. I am interested. Not that I go to the library but. Ah! and bla bla bla!

By point we walked along with Kelly I said, look, Mike, you know, of course, in Anthropology I believe in extraterrestrials, Sasquatch, and that we have had higher technology on Earth than we have today. Oh, yeah, well, how far back do you think we have had higher technology than now. 6 thousand years ago, 12 thousand years ago? I can't recall numbers he offered verbatim. I think I recall a 6 in there somewhere. 60 thousand years ago, no matter, I said: Sure.

Then I set him off, which is sad always. I said: It is proven. He cannot hear nor reason, he thinks we are in this marble game and fudging is fine if you can get away with fudging. I get irritated because I prefer freedom with my own thoughts. At a point I yelled:

Fuck that shit, that doesn't have a goddamn thing to do with what I am talking about!....At that point, his oratory on actual "proof," I had brought in Sasquatch, because that is easy, a certain anthropologist at the U. of Idaho, Jeff Meldrum, who is also a foot specialist and did plaster casts of a critter with a foot once broken but healed over. Meldrum, alive today, has shown exactly the broken bone of foot and so forth, on the Web,and I had attempted telling Mike there are many such studied types doing these plaster casts and naturally they know all about snow and mud and are way off beaten paths. I should by now have known better. When I yelled fuck that shit Mike was in this "story" of following these prints in snow off beaten path thinking it human and wondering how can a human be out barefooted in sub zero etc, and Mike catches up and sees a bear, something about said bear stood up....I was not hearing him then, fuck it. I already knew inexpert folks have seen bear prints in snow where the black bear has placed hind feet into paw prints thus looking like longer prints. Humans are bipedal and a large Sasquatch has bigger foot prints than an Alaskan grizzly, biggest brown bear. Whichever, Mike O. is out here being a scientist and talking about his old age and now he is studying paleontology and if he prefers to think I am without education of authority, hell, let him have at it. He does not expect to make another twenty years, anyway. Too, I do never have education of authority. Authority of puny man no damn good. I am a seer. Get used to it. The Art of Knowing.

Geoffrey, am glad you look at Debbie Lusignan sometimes. She, and Madrea, are as smart as people get to be, without madness like I survive, eh. Debbie's latest is: Kim Dotcom No Magic Bullet on Seth Rich Case. Debbie is lively in this one and had me laughing. She is extraordinary, besides always correct.

Love,
Bill

Barron and Michele,

Thus past week Packy and Bill exchanged yet on different frequencies. A day or two back Mike Blackbird and I talked a bit on old friends passed on, consensus being these who went had some particularly damaging habits physically. This had me thinking of Packy, who has done all this, too. Stress (severe paranoia, severe created grudges), overeating, over consumption of drink, speed, smack and so on. Maybe Packy did not do smack. He did if slyly to me admit to speed (way more damaging than smack), which clarified his behavior post 1980. Am paused to wonder does he not care to visit, maybe he is too fat or still smoking packaged killer cigarettes, and maybe Bill will be disgusted. That, he prefers magic bowel movements into a telephone if somebody will hold phone to ear a couple and more hours.

Few years back at Lyla's John G. visited and said of his last experience with Packy on phone, John had to go do something, and he did not try breaking into monologue but just did what he needed to do.

He returned and picked up phone and Packy was going strong. John G. said: It is bizarre.

Yas, yas, many of us from this dimension are gone to another.

Tiddle C.: What does it all mean. Judge R D H. III: Nothing means shit! Oh, Hatch is alive and looks healthy. But in order to become a lawyer and a judge he fought peyote. Went schizoid, fearful of even smoking pot. Tries now days to not remember TG is American literature. He speaks strangely, and no telling.

Re.TG: How so many women like it. For sure. OK, but not Bonnie Blackbird, whom I have turned to tears many times, and settling out here into quarters she has given me, I see I have been insensitive.

All my life, and enough on that. Packy of TALES FROM THE TEXAS GANG: A man has got to fuck or run or fight or something. OK, my Dear Reader. To the Ladies. To the Mothers. To the Whores.

Jaaiee, caramba!

I love that. Trying to not digress. Excuse me, ladies and gents, now where was I.

Schizoid Nation has been against Bill Blackbird making a kind of a living. Dogs in thicket of an Austin river but ample food. I never could tell would a singular sort of person relax to read TG.

When from the Drag in Austin I handed out much of the original 2000, people were coming back to me. My grandmother loved this book!

Anybody can fucking read it. Bikers, grandmothers. I am literate.

Both Packy and RD are a bit slow there. Wives would tell me I am not like what they had heard from their husbands and their husbands' friends.

Late Ken Kesey I had sent a copy and Packy asked him what he thought. Kesey and I are on the same side. Kesey: It is good but it is too hard to read. I did meet Kesey at an Austin gathering and we passed pipe and got along, then came wannabes, and "we" had no chance to talk. Same when I met Ginsberg but am apollogetic I did scare witless Ginsberg. I will say, Kesey did not believe TG hard to read.

He but claimed so. He wanted to milk but his own cow. Oh, possibly something got lost in this long car ride in Packy's translation back to his oldest friend Bill.

This second printing, an actual publisher, without contacts, Jeff P., I made certain this edition had the William Burroughs II letter to me, on TALES FROM THE TEXAS GANG etc.

"But I can't even get Grove Press to accept my son's novels."

I and Bill III got along, his couple novels did get out there, beatnik lit. He admired I had a pack of eight feral dogs in my pickup. He was drinking on a liver transplant, oh, beer, day and evening. Several more years.

Sounds like you two are busy enough enjoying this life together. Am glad. Keep it up, sacred.

I tell Packy to not feel sorry for self and ho hum, I have this too. Nobody to talk to about Pedogate. Fucking nuts gone to dynamite any day now. Too strange for me to grasp, and said I have heard of it years now. Some cosmic disease, what in Hell. Thick, thick shit. We hope we can grab this legally before we and nations launch nukes. Grab it legally. Gasp. Legally, ok. Or not legally.

Just snatch this. No further dodge fucking Jesus. Jesus fucking son of Mary if you are no help I alone myself will come to kill, I will figure some way, revelation, revelation, revelation. Medicine dog, Medicine Dog, I am here.

I have told of a few good names, a few and there is many. Not enough yet. USA has got to be stirred, stirred to addled fire ants. I can't manage any exaggeration longer now though instinctively I be understating. Fucking wailing nuts. OK, will give it to understatement. For a moment. Can this planet live. Either way.

Where is this Packy G.? Who is he? Bill does not care how fat is Packy without our olden communication is utterly killed. Yah, if he is still on cigarettes he needs cut off a pinky. Time to move out now.

And so on. My God is Medicine Dog. Choyota is in here whom immature Medicine Dog was not always nice to and she is chipper, senses Real World. MEDICINE DAWG! DAWG! WE KILL!

Love,
Bill

***

Well, then, the other morning I stopped in to that restaurant in Northeast, the one where Kaitylyn used to work. She drew the chalkboard menus and Prince Hope said he met her there, but I don't know if she ever said anything about that.

Blake also works at The Friendly Face, and I guess now he's in charge of Geronimo Day, but on Saturdays he and Rachel come in and bake and sell "Rachel's Pies," so I decided to stop on in.

I guess Jorge and Roswell are still on the farm, visited quite often, I'm certain, by Rachel and Blake. The house has not burned down, yet. I'm glad I was wrong with that prediction.

There goes Washington. Wonder where he got the bike?

I guess he gives talks at that one "Vets Club," steals what he needs at the C-store, I'm actually not really sure. He told somebody he's got an interview at White Castle. He's a go-getter, at times, after noon, that Washington.

Prince Hope well, you get three guesses, not at a Bisbee radio station doing the midnight to four shift or podcasts five afternoons a week on the Anger Internet Network. He's not the minister of doom anymore or whatever the hell that was. Anyway, I don't see his face on the big screens during the fly-overs. Now it's some high school kid.

Well, all to be fucking continued, I'm sure.

Korey was there, dressed as a pirate or a dancer, I'm not sure, but he was in disguise and he was eating pie at a window table. He doesn't make eye contact, but it's his way of staying in touch. That's what I think.

Actually, I lied, I did hear two homeless guys on the street not that long ago talking about how Prince Hope is going to start another Farewell Tour and how they knew somebody's cousin who could get tickets.

I still see him around town. Korey. I don't think he knows who I am anymore, which is the way it should be. I'm not there for him, never was. He is there for me. It's good to see that look in his eye, to know that somebody is still angry and fighting, not everyone is scared. Well, I'm sure he's scared, but he's also angry.

And to me that means something.

He's No. 7 on the current FBI charts. Not bad, but I'm sure he thinks he can do better.

Blake said Korey talks to him. He mentioned one time Washington wanted to team up again and do something, really stick it to the man, and I guess Korey just said, "I'll take my chances alone."

I kind of like that.

He's not going to try to "get better," make his way back into society, get an associate arts degree and eventually when he's forty-six have a yard and a gas grill on the West Side. He's a CRUSHER. Wow, you gotta love that. But he's gonna fuckin' die. No way it will work. But, you know, what the fuck?

I was at the funeral, for Evey.

I remembered talking to her once during one of those visits to the farm.

I asked her how do you get your respect that everyone needs to live to not be depressed? And she said, what? Well, I said, people need respect from the society, even if you are on the edge, you need some kind of respect, self-respect, to not be all the time depressed, at least that's what I think, don't you?

She said, "Oh! Ed Chigliak, battling the demons of external validation!"

And she smiled and I had no idea what she was talking about.

She said, "I don't eat, the more skinny I get it makes me feel better, and running helps, and medicine. And sometimes I drink. I did quit smoking."

And I thought, my Lord, sorry for askin', I really did.

She said, "I think we're doing the right thing."

"But how do you, you know, keep going," I said because I am really a good reporter. I really am, nobody believes me, but I am. I want the story, no matter who I hurt."

"I'm as surprised as you are," she said.

Wow, all these folks from The Friendly Face Facility. Lots of them brought Evey's CRUSHER Queen of Hearts and dropped them into the hole.

They sang "feed the birds, tuppins a bag, tuppins, tuppins."

I don't know man, but before I was all with Jim, take the fucking money, but after hearing that, I don't know, I might feed the birds, all day long.

Just sayin', ya know?

And while they were there they stopped at all the other graves, Jim, Lara, Kaitylyn, then the big group moved up to the top of the hill and gathered around Geronimo's grave.

I stood there, right in with them and closed my eyes.

It's weird but I could see him, Geronimo. I didn't even know him, but I've heard about him for so long I pretty much have made up this picture in my mind … and he was right there with us. And so was Josephine Custer, his sister, The Beautiful Indian Maiden Heroine, nobody calls her that, I do. I saw her too. I did. I fucking did. She wore a wry grin. I hope she's all right. She was there with Geronimo and Lara, Kaitylyn, Jim. I could feel it, man. It was so weird. And I didn't want to open my eyes and I didn't want to leave.

Oh, not to change the subject, but I have a little house now. I don't really know anybody. I thought I'd throw a party to meet people and I didn't know anyone to invite, so I invited the neighbor's dog. I'm starting out slow. I'm also writing a new book. If I don't I'll die, not that there's anything wrong with that.

That's what I think. But it would be more of a novel, a made-up story. I might die and not finish it. I always worry about that. But what if I live? So, yeah, it's called "The Country That Never Was." I've got notes for it. Starts out with somebody singing "American The Beautiful" with some of the wrong words, like we grow up our whole lives singing in our head some pop song and it's the wrong words, something like that.

The most amazing things happen slowly, gradually, hardly even notice, a grind, like a life, like raising children, like … and then, just wow. We think it's cool when someone is away for a long time, like disappears for years in the woods, or spends a long time in a monastery, maybe a whole life. He went away because of something terrible. Anyway, those are my notes. Wish me luck. I'm gonna fucking need it.

Well, here's what I think happened to ol' Geronimo Gerry.
…
He could have been President. I really think he could.
This is America.
What if we faked like we found something from 9/11 … They had just watched this show on the History Channel or something

... I wonder what would happen if we did that ... we'd find out who THEY are probly, right? *Let's do it.*

I don't know, man, said Jim.

And so they did.

They made a ticket. Geronimo drew an airplane and they wrote some shit on the little oblong piece of construction paper. Put it in plastic like you do a valuable baseball card.

He didn't let anyone see it very long or hold it. It was a mystery, a legend, a story, but everybody believed in it.

And probly Jim started to believe it. The ticket wasn't the reason for the rebellion. Geronimo was the reason. Tuppins was the reason. Jim probly forgot all about the fucking ticket.

But Geronimo.

He never did. He kept going. He wanted to find out what was what. He was no dummy. He wanted to find out what would happen to someone who had something they wanted. And he found out. And now he knows.

At least that's what I think happened. You might think something else and you would probably be right.

I saw Actually at White Castle a few days later and he told me it was so weird, he said.

"At about that same time as Evey's funeral, I didn't go 'cause I have a life now, I was waiting on a customer and I told him that I felt something in The Woo, not a disruption, more of a building, a growing stronger like thing, and I told him, yeah, man, that is a thing, The Woo, man. And I said, no, stop, you can't Google it. It's the fucking Woo, man. And he left. No, I can't get fired. I'm the manager."

That's what Actually said. And BTW, he is now starting to call himself Siri. He says Actually is so over. I said, "PRPQT." I just made it up. It doesn't mean shit, but Siri, that's cool, sort of an eastern thing.

Blake works at The Friendly Face Facility. I said that?

Rachel came back after she ran away for a little while and they live in Northeast. They make "Rachel's Pies," and sell some and give some to the homeless. I didn't say that part.

Well, I was sitting at the counter eating to-die-for "Blueberry Bomb" when Blake literally came over and said, "you got to hear this."

He said that somebody knows someone who works overnight at a group home, somewhere in Saint Paul, there must be literally hundreds of those, you'd never know it, and the person was up late.

It's an awake overnight, and while the troops were outside marching on the wet pavement, and doing like they do, singing, chanting, "Good God Y'all … Hoooh!" … well she was watching Brooke's documentary, "Brooke The Spy," the spy one, you know, by PH Prods The Red Unit. I guess it's been airing on public access.

And the next day or whenever she comes up to her friend who also works at the same home and she says something like, "We need to fight against all this … we need to save the country … we need to go to the barricades … and we need to show them we're not afraid … and I think so and so and them would do it … somebody has to be a real superhero, actually change the world, why not us, huh?

"Huh?"

And her friend, she says …, "Yeah.

"Yeah, we could do that."

The battle ... has to begin here. In America.
The only institution more powerful than the U.S.
government is American civil society ... You have access to the Imperial Palace and the Emperor's cham-
bers. Empire's conquests are being carried
out in your name.

— Arundhati Roy

www.ingramcontent.com/pod-product-compliance
Lightning Source LLC
Chambersburg PA
CBHW070834120626
46556CB00002B/751